Mrs. Malory and Any Man's Death

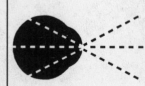

This Large Print Book carries the
Seal of Approval of N.A.V.H.

A SHEILA MALORY MYSTERY

MRS. MALORY AND ANY MAN'S DEATH

HAZEL HOLT

THORNDIKE PRESS
A part of Gale, Cengage Learning

GALE
CENGAGE Learning™

Detroit • New York • San Francisco • New Haven, Conn • Waterville, Maine • London

GALE
CENGAGE Learning™

Thorndike Press® Large Print Mystery.
The text of this Large Print edition is unabridged.
Other aspects of the book may vary from the original edition.
Set in 16 pt. Plantin.
Printed on permanent paper.

LIBRARY OF CONGRESS CATALOGING-IN-PUBLICATION DATA

Holt, Hazel, 1928–
  Mrs. Malory and any man's death : a Sheila Malory mystery / by Hazel Holt. — Large print ed.
      p. cm.
  Originally published: New York : Obsidian, 2009.
  ISBN-13: 978-1-4104-2487-7 (alk. paper)
  ISBN-10: 1-4104-2487-1 (alk. paper)
  1. Malory, Sheila (Fictitious character)—Fiction. 2. Women detectives—England—Fiction. 3. England—Fiction. 4. Large type books. I. Title.
  PR6058.O473M749 2010
  823'.914—dc22   2009049408

Published in 2010 by arrangement with NAL Signet, a member of Penguin Group (USA) Inc.

Printed in the United States of America
1 2 3 4 5 6 7 14 13 12 11 10

For Laura
With love and thanks

Any man's death diminishes me,
because I am involved in Mankind.
— John Donne

CHAPTER ONE

"If you ask me," Anthea said, "I think it's a *great* mistake."

"Oh, I don't know," I said mildly. "They are sisters after all, and they always used to get on well together."

"Years ago. Things are very different now. Rachel's used to having her own home and doing things her own way. And you remember how she always used to want to run everything."

This, coming from Anthea, who runs most things in Taviscombe, was pretty rich. "I'm sure they'll work it out," I said. "After all, they both live alone, and if Rachel wants to come back here now that Alastair's dead, it makes a lot of sense."

"I can't think why Phyllis stayed on in that enormous house after her father died. She'd have been much better off in a nice bungalow."

"Oh, but it's been the family home for

generations," I said. "Her grandfather built it before the Great War. It was one of the first new houses to be built in Mere Barton — I remember Mother saying there was quite a bit of excitement about it at the time. I know Phyll couldn't bear to live anywhere else, and I expect Rachel has many happy memories of it."

"Well, it's still far too big for the two of them," Anthea persisted. "I thought as much when Dr. Gregory was alive and it was just him and Phyllis."

"Oh, he'd never have moved," I said. "He loved the house and being in the village, especially after he retired; he was so much a part of the place. I must say, I couldn't imagine the village without him."

"Anyway, why does Rachel want to come back after all those years in Scotland? I'd have thought she'd have made her own life up there."

"Inverness was Alastair's home," I said, "and when he was offered a practice there, of course he took it. I'm sure she was quite happy while he was alive, but I don't think she would have wanted to stay there without him."

"But what about the son? Where's he?"

"Jamie? Oh, he's gone off to Africa somewhere — Médecins sans Frontières —

something like that. So Rachel's quite on her own."

There was a brief silence while Anthea considered and filed away the information she'd acquired.

"So, when's this welcome home party, then?" she asked.

"Rachel's due here next week, and I expect she'll want time to settle in, but Phyll thought she'd just let us know what she's got planned."

"Well, I hope it's not on a Wednesday," Anthea said. "I'm never free on Wednesdays."

"I'm sure Phyll will remember that," I said.

Rachel Craig was an old school friend, part of our special group.

"It'll be nice to see her again," Rosemary said. "It's ages since she's been back in Taviscombe."

"Well, it's quite a journey from Inverness, even if you fly. She did come back for her mother's funeral, though. If you remember, she couldn't get away for Dr. Gregory's because Alastair was so ill then. Poor Phyll was very upset about that."

"Oh, Phyll always put her father before anyone else," Rosemary said. "Look at the way she gave up a perfectly good job to come back and look after him when her mother died."

"She never seemed to me to be that keen on a career — not like Rachel."

"She could have been head of her department if she'd stayed on at that school in Portsmouth."

"I suppose so, but she always said she really only liked the teaching — and I can see she'd be a splendid teacher — but she'd be hopeless with a lot of paperwork. Rachel, now, was Alastair's nurse-practitioner and pretty well ran the whole thing. I only hope she finds enough scope in Mere Barton for all her energies!"

"Well, if Anthea's right," Rosemary said, "and she does intend to run the village, she'll find pretty stiff opposition from Annie."

Annie Roberts used to be the district nurse, and even though she's retired, she's still greatly in demand for unofficial consultations. She sees herself — rightly — as the hub of the village, living where she does right in the middle of the main street, next to the village shop. The door of Willow Cottage usually stands open so that Annie can see who's passing and engage them in conversation. She's the repository of a great deal of information about what goes on in the village, but she never gossips. "Patient confidentiality," she always says when asked about anything, pressing her lips tightly together to indicate the degree of her integrity. In addition to all that, she runs most of the village activities — she's in charge of the village hall, president of the Women's Institute, treasurer of the parochial church council, and it's Annie who makes the collection for Poppy Day and other flag days for worthy causes. "Well, I've got the time, you see, now that I'm retired," she says, ignoring the fact that a large proportion of the population of Mere Barton are also retired and longing for something to occupy their newly acquired leisure. Though, of course, she is perfectly happy to enroll them as her lieutenants, carrying out her orders, as it were, and, as yet, no one has had the courage to challenge her leadership. Not that she is a formidable figure — she's barely five feet. She has, however, the immense energy that small people often seem to have, and to see her about the village on some ploy or another is like watching a purposeful darting insect.

I laughed. "Oh, I think Rachel knows enough not to take on Annie."

"Or Anthea at Brunswick Lodge?" Rosemary suggested. Brunswick Lodge, a large eighteenth-century house, is the social and cultural center of Taviscombe, and Anthea's own particular fiefdom.

"Don't! That's a terrible thought! But, actually, Rachel is far too tactful to make any sort of overt takeover. If she wanted to, she'd do it so subtly that the person taken over from would actually thank her! Do you remember at school how she always got her own way without seeming to try?"

"Oh well," Rosemary said, "it'll be interesting to see what happens."

Phyll rang about ten days later.

"She's dying to see you all," she said, "so could you come next Tuesday? I thought a lunchtime thing would be best — a lot of people don't really like driving at night. Twelve or twelve thirty. Drinks and a few odds and ends to eat, nothing formal. Not a lot of people, mostly neighbors from the village and you and Rosemary, of course."

"That sounds lovely," I said. "I'll look forward to it."

Rosemary and I arranged to go together. "If you think it's going on too long," she said, "just give me a nod and I'll say I've got to go and collect Alex from school."

The road to Mere Barton is very narrow,

with virtually no passing places, and any encounter with a lorry or a tractor means having to back up a long way with your head uncomfortably screwed over your shoulder.

"I must say I'm grateful not to have to drive down this road in the dark," I said. "And thank goodness for a solid Edwardian house with a proper drive so there's plenty of space to park!"

Higher Barton, as its name indicates, stands on a slight eminence just outside the village. It is very handsome, its red brick mellowed by time and with a multiplicity of lovingly crafted architectural adornments that would actually justify that house agents' favorite phrase, "many period features." There were already several cars there, as some of the local residents had elected to drive the short distance from the village, and I parked beside the shiny new Range Rover that belonged to Diana Parker. Her husband, Toby, is a Member of Parliament with a London constituency, but Diana chooses to live down here on the farm that used to be his family home. Not that it's a farm now, just a done-over farmhouse, several fields and stabling where Diana keeps her horses.

"All the usual suspects," Rosemary murmured as we went into the drawing room.

"I think you know everybody," Phyll said, leading us forward. "Rachel, here's Sheila and Rosemary."

Rachel never really seems to change. Obviously she's grown older, as we all have, but her hair is dark and her face unlined — all, I'm quite sure, without any artificial aids — and she still has the air of relaxed confidence that marked her out even as a schoolgirl.

"How lovely to see you both again." She came towards us, her hands outstretched and with that particularly sweet smile I remembered so well, and I felt a wave of affection, as I felt Rosemary did too, as she embraced us. Rachel always was a special person.

We exchanged a few disjointed remarks and Rachel said, "We can't chat properly now, and there's so much I want to catch up on. Shall we have lunch at the Buttery, for old time's sake? How about Friday?"

As schoolgirls the three of us always used to go to the Buttery after games (though it wasn't called the Buttery then — I think it was the Periwinkle) to drink hot chocolate and complain about being forced to participate in athletic activities.

Rachel went away to talk to the little group who were standing beside a table where Phyllis's odds and ends to eat were laid out; though, since she is a splendid cook, they were considerably more than that.

"Come and have some of these gorgeous crostini," Judith Lamb called out to us. "I don't know how Phyllis manages to do all these wonderful things. The spread she put on for the village hall Christmas party was fabulous!"

Judith is the widow of an accountant — they both came here from Birmingham when he retired. He died a few years ago, and Judith lives in the cottage next to Annie's and is her most enthusiastic helper. She, too, is small and purposeful, but built with fuller lines. She has a round face perched on a round body, and to the fanciful eye resembles an old-fashioned cottage loaf.

"Here." William Faber offered a plate. "Do try some of these excellent miniature pizzas — such a good idea!"

William Faber is the rector of All Saints, the handsome village church, and has the care of two other parishes. He likes to be called Father William (though I do find my thoughts fly instantly and inappropriately to Lewis Carroll when I hear him addressed in this way) and has, as they say, spiked up the services (in the face of some opposition —

appeals having (been made to the bishop) in all three parish. He can quite frequently be heard giving witty, inspirational talks on the radio in the Thought for the Day slot and is, consequently, very popular in the village.

A group of other people now came into the room: Fred and Ellen Tucker, who have the one remaining farm in the village; Maurice Sanders, who used to be some sort of civil servant but who, with his wife, Margaret, now keeps the village shop; George Prosser, a retired navy captain; Jim and Mary Fletcher (he had been a bank manager and she was a librarian); Lewis and Naomi Chapman (he still works as an anesthetist and she was engaged in some sort of medical research); and, finally, ushering them all through the door like an efficient sheepdog, Annie Roberts.

"We all walked up from the village," Annie said. "It's such a lovely day."

The room, large as it was, suddenly seemed very full of people and I retreated, with my plate of food, to one of the window seats where I was joined by Lewis Chapman.

"I'll wait for the scrum to subside," he said, smiling, "before I attack the food."

Lewis is a really nice man, a cheerful soul

with a jolly out⸍ ng disposition, in contrast to his wife's ⸍ust⸍re and withdrawn manner. I never feel entirely at ease with Naomi. I always think of that description of Katisha in *The Mikado* — "as hard as a bone with a mind of her own" — and there's something of Katisha's imperiousness there too. I always feel she's judging me . . . and usually finding me wanting.

"I'm really sorry about poor old Alastair," Lewis said. "We go back a long way; we did part of our training together at Barts. But it must have been a dreadful time for Rachel — he was ill for so long and he needed a lot of nursing. I must say," he continued, looking across the room, "she looks pretty good after all she's had to go through."

"Rachel's always been tough," I said, "mentally and physically, right from when we were at school together. She always coped, no matter what. That's why I'm glad she's back here with Phyll. Poor Phyll. I don't think she's really got over her father's death, even now."

"He was a good age."

"I know, but I suppose we all expect our parents to be immortal."

"Ah, there you are, Lewis." Naomi came toward us holding her plate, glass and handbag in the sort of elegant and effortless way that I can never achieve. "Are you getting some food?"

Lewis got up obediently and went over to the table while Naomi joined me.

"So, Sheila," she said, "and what are you writing now?"

"Writing? Oh, nothing special, just a few reviews."

"Such a pity. I greatly enjoyed your book on Mrs. Gaskell." She gave me what might pass for a smile. "We shouldn't let our talents rust as we get older."

"I never seem to have the time," I said, disconcerted as I frequently am by Naomi's style of conversation, "what with the house and the animals and the children."

"I find that one can usually make the time if it's something one *really* wants to do." She bit neatly into a vol-au-vent without, I noticed with loathing, scattering shards of puff pastry as other people do.

It was with some relief that I saw Annie Roberts making her way towards us.

"Sheila," she said. "Just the person I want to see." My heart sank because I knew immediately that there was something she wanted me to do — and one never says no to Annie. "Just come over and have a word with me and Ellen. It's about the Book."

The Book, always referred to with a

capital letter by those involved with it, was Annie's latest project. Realizing that there'd been a proliferation of village history books — not meager little brochures, but substantial, glossy publications — with documents going back (if possible) to the Domesday Book and ancient photographs and reminiscences, Annie decided that Mere Barton should not be left out. Unfortunately, to produce such a volume it's necessary to have suitable material (especially pictorial records), and the only people able to provide that would be those whose families had lived in the village for generations. Mere Barton was singularly lacking in such people. Of the original inhabitants only Fred and Ellen Tucker, Phyll and Rachel, Toby Parker and Annie herself remained.

Annie detached Ellen from the group she had been happily engaged with.

"Right, then. I thought you two ought to get together," Annie said. "Sheila's our local author so she's obviously the person to help you, Ellen, and I thought we could all meet sometime next week and get things moving. We've got some material — that stuff of Fred's, for instance, Ellen — and I've got all those photos of my grandfather's. Sheila will be able to tell you what we can use, and I've got a lot of ideas we can all of us follow up. So shall we say next Monday morning, ten o'clock at my cottage?"

Ellen and I looked helplessly at each other and silently nodded our agreement to this arrangement.

"Right," Annie said. "I'll see you then. Oh, there's Diana. I'm sure Toby has all sorts of family things that we could use. I'll get her to look them out, and I'll have a word with him when he comes down."

She dived across the room and Ellen and I looked at each other and smiled.

"Poor Diana," I said. "And poor Toby too. Perhaps he'll take refuge in the House where she can't get at him."

"I'm sorry, Sheila," Ellen said. "I'm sure you didn't want to get roped in for this, but I really would be grateful if you could lend a hand. It's not my sort of thing at all and I haven't the faintest idea how to go about it."

"Well, apart from being resentful at being pushed around by Annie, I'd really quite like to have a look at the material. I love old photos and things like that so it will be a pleasure." I saw Rosemary making little waving gestures to me across the room. "Oh, I think Rosemary wants to go, but I'll see you at Annie's on Monday."

Driving home, I told Rosemary about my

involvement in the Book.

"It might be interesting," I said, "if only I didn't feel so cross at being manipulated by Annie!"

"Well, you know what she's like — she's got the whole village under her thumb; I wish I knew how she manages it! Still, she does get things done; I'll say that for her."

I cautiously overtook a tractor with an unsteady load of silage. "I wonder what happened to Anthea." I said. "Do you think she's ill?"

"And, did you notice? Nobody asked about her. I wonder," Rosemary continued thoughtfully, "if she was actually invited."

CHAPTER TWO

Foss, my Siamese, in his endless quest for entertainment, has invented a new ploy. When I go upstairs he rushes past and lies across the stair in front of me. This means that I either have to step over him (difficult because they are steep cottage stairs) or pay him the attention he requires by stroking him. This continues all the way up the stairs (mercifully he doesn't do it for the down-ward journey). I suppose I should have sharply discouraged him when he started it, but because he thought of it all by himself, and because (of course) I'm a fool about animals, I go along with it even though it makes going upstairs a very slow business indeed. This, and the fact that it took me ages to find anywhere to park in the village (the main street is always full of people who have driven the short distance to the village shop), meant that I was late getting to Annie's.

I went in through the open front door and found Annie and Ellen seated at the large round table that takes up the greater part of her small sitting room.

"Oh, there you are," Annie said. "We'd almost given you up."

I made my apologies, aware that I'd started off on the wrong foot and would have to be especially cooperative to make up.

"Well, sit down now that you're here and see what you think of these photos that Ellen's brought."

A collection of old sepia pictures was spread out, mostly of agricultural pursuits — harvesting with open wooden carts and heavy horses, ploughing (the horses again), people in old-fashioned clothes, holding farm implements, standing self-consciously in front of groups of sheep or cattle — the collective memory of one family pinned down in time.

"Aren't they splendid!" I said enthusiastically. "And look at this one of the village street; all the cottages look quite shabby, very different from now when they've all been done up."

"Oh well," Ellen said, "the village is full of off-comers now — retired people or commuters. Everything's been buzzed up. Fred's father said that when he was a boy it was a proper working village. There was a tailor, a baker, a wheelwright, a shoemaker, a blacksmith, and an alehouse."

"An alehouse?" I asked. "Where the hotel is now?"

"Bless you, no." Ellen laughed. "It was at Rose Cottage, just down from here — you knocked on the door and handed in your jug and they filled it with ale."

"I remember old Johnny Yates at the bakery," Annie said. "When I was a child he'd bake your pies for you in his big oven. And the blacksmith's only been gone a few years — when Ted Andrews died."

"Still, his son, Geoff, has kept on the business," Ellen said. "Well, he's just a farrier now and drives around with a portable forge in the back of his truck."

"I suppose that's something," I said, "but it's very sad, to think of how things have changed, and not necessarily for the better."

"Well, and that's what this book's all about," Annie said briskly, "putting it all down so it isn't forgotten."

Called to order, we went back to sorting through the photos.

"Well," I said, "it's a splendid start. Do we have the promise of any more?"

"I asked Diana to see what she can find of

26

Toby's family," Annie said. "They've been in the village for generations — gentleman farmers, is what they used to be called. I must get her moving on that. There are all mine, of course. I didn't get them out today because there's still a lot of stuff in a chest upstairs and I wanted to see what I've got."

"And I suppose there should be some from Rachel and Phyll," I said. "Dr. Gregory's family goes back quite a long way. Has anyone asked them?"

"Oh, I've got Rachel on to that. She's more organized than Phyllis," Annie said approvingly. "And Ellen here has some old newspaper cuttings and objects that could be interesting."

"That's splendid," I said. "Lovely to have things like that. I wish we did."

"Oh, nobody ever throws anything away in our house," Ellen said. "The place is full of stuff. Honestly, trying to keep it clean and tidy is a nightmare!"

"Now, Sheila," Annie said. "I've asked Father William to let you have access to the church records so you can deal with all that side of things, and I want you to write a history of the village — it was mentioned in the Domesday Book, you know."

My heart sank. "A *history*?"

"It can be quite short, and I'm sure you

can find a lot of material in the County Records Office."

"Yes," I agreed despondently. "I'm sure I can."

Ellen gave me a sympathetic glance. "Well, then, if that's all, I've got to be on my way. Fred's moving the sheep up into the top field and he'll need me to lend him a hand."

She got up and I looked at my watch and said hastily, "Oh, is that the time? I really ought to be going too."

"Well," Annie said disapprovingly, "we haven't got nearly as much done as I thought we would. Now, Sheila, do keep me up-to-date with how you're getting on, and, Ellen, if you can look out those old farm implements soon, Jim Fletcher said he'd photograph them."

"Yes, of course," I said.

"As soon as I can," Ellen said as we both backed quickly out of the room.

When we were outside, we walked a little way along the village street together and Ellen said, "Do you fancy coming back for a coffee?"

"What about the sheep?" I asked.

She laughed. "I always go prepared with some excuse when Annie corners me like that. I advise you to do the same!"

"How very sensible," I said admiringly.

"Yes, please, I'd love to come."

"We'll go down in your car. I walked up because I know how impossible it is to park anywhere near the shop in the morning."

I looked back along the village street. It was lined with a variety of vehicles and with people standing about in the middle of the road chatting, oblivious of a large van trying to make a delivery and a dilapidated Land Rover attempting to make its way through, with two Jack Russell terriers, their paws on the open windows, barking furiously.

"I do see what you mean," I said.

We retrieved my car from the driveway of the Exmoor Hotel at the edge of the village, where I'd left it in desperation earlier on, and drove down to Blackwell Farm. A couple of sheepdogs came bounding out to meet us, with Fred Tucker coming in behind them.

"So you managed to get away, then," he said. "Hello, Sheila. So she's got you roped in as well, then."

"I'm afraid so," I said ruefully. "I suppose I did sort of offer, but I'd no idea what I'd let myself in for — hours in the County Records Office in Taunton for a start!"

"Never offer to do anything for Annie," Ellen said. "You'll always get more than you bargain for. Come on in to the kitchen, Sheila, and I'll put the kettle on. Do you want one too, Fred?"

"Can you fill a flask for me? Dan and I are going to put up that new pig arc."

"Dan is working for you now, then?" I asked. Dan, their youngest son, has just left school; Mark, the older one, is away in the army.

"He's helping out for a bit before he goes to agricultural college next year," Ellen said.

"And then he'll come back here?"

"If there's anything to come back to," Fred said. "I don't know why I bother with pigs — they don't fetch enough to cover the feed. If the wheat prices keep up, I can put some more fields down to arable, but a lot of the land, on the edge of the moor, that's only fit for sheep, and they're no more profitable than the pigs."

He sat down opposite me at the kitchen table and seemed prepared to continue to air his grievances.

"Fred's always been one to look on the gloomy side," Ellen said, spooning some coffee powder into a jug, filling it with hot water and milk, pouring it into a flask, and screwing the top down tightly. "There you are, then," she said, picking up a packet of biscuits from the table and giving it to him along with the flask. "That'll see you and Dan all right for a bit."

A young man put his head round the door and called out, "Are you coming, Dad? Those weaners'll be here in an hour and we haven't got that pen ready for them."

"I'll be off, then." Fred got up reluctantly. "Nice to see you, Sheila. Don't let Annie work you to death."

Ellen laughed. "Poor old Fred. He does love a chat and we don't get many visitors he can let off steam to."

She pushed a cup of coffee towards me. "It's only instant," she said. "I gave up the proper stuff years ago — too much effort." She opened another packet of biscuits and put some on a plate. "And I never seem to have time for baking anymore."

"It must be pretty hard," I said.

"Market prices are dreadful and the feed goes up all the time. I do all the paperwork now — there's no way Fred could spare the time. I mean, in the old days there'd be two or three men working on the farm, but now, even with the machinery, and *that* costs the earth, it's still a lot of work for the two of us."

"Dan must be a great help."

"He's a good lad, and I do hope Fred's just being gloomy and we *can* manage to carry on somehow."

"Oh, you must!" I exclaimed. "You're the last farm in the village. Everyone would be devastated if you had to give up."

"Not everyone," Ellen said. "We get all these complaints."

"Complaints?"

"Oh, the tractors leave mud on the road; it isn't nice to have trailers with manure going through the village; the bird scarers are too noisy; the pigs smell — that sort of thing."

"But that's ridiculous!" I exclaimed. "How can they complain about country living?"

"That's it, of course," Ellen said bitterly. "They don't want to live in the country — they want to live in some idyllic rural spot with people just like themselves and no nasty noises or smells."

"Not all of them, surely," I said.

"No. It's the Fletchers, really. The others are more or less all right — the Sanderses are quite sympathetic. Though, mind you, I don't think they realized what they were taking on with the village shop."

"People have a dream," I said, "and I suppose it's inevitable that reality sometimes gives them a real awakening."

"I must say, though," Ellen said, "that Maurice has been very clever."

"Really?"

"He's worked out that people in the village are going to go to the supermarket for their main shopping, just for cheapness, and he knew he couldn't make a living relying on them coming to him if they'd just run out of sugar or something, so he's specialized in fancy foods and deli things. They cost the earth, but all the newcomers are well-off and can easily afford them. They think it's rather smart to have a speciality shop right here in the village — they're always boasting about it to their friends when they come down from London."

"Well, good for him. Come to think of it, I seem to remember he stocked a rather nice smoked eel pâté. I must call in on my way back to get some." I took a biscuit and said, "It really is awful to think how the village has changed — even in the past few years."

"What really gets me," Ellen said sadly, "is not having the school bus stopping here anymore. There's not a single child in the village now — not since Dan left school."

"That's terrible."

"Oh, people's grandchildren come to stay in the school holidays, but it's not the same."

"No continuity," I said.

"No. When these villagers die they'll

simply be replaced by other people who've retired and so it'll go on."

"Well," I said encouragingly, "your Dan will marry and have children one day."

"I hope so — if we haven't been driven away by the Fletchers." She laughed. "Listen to me — I'm beginning to sound like Fred!"

When I left Riverside I managed to park quite near the village shop. I looked in through the window to make sure Annie wasn't there. Fortunately she wasn't, though there were quite a few other people in there and a great deal of conversation, though not, as far as I could see, much trade being done. I suppose Mere Barton is lucky to have a village shop and, I suppose, it's mainly thanks to the off-comers who can afford to pay fancy prices to keep it going. When I went in I gradually identified some faces that I knew: Mary Fletcher, Diana Parker, George Prosser and Judith Lamb, who, perched on a stool by the counter, looked as if she was a permanent fixture there. She greeted me warmly.

"Sheila — fancy seeing you again so soon!"

I explained my involvement with the village book. "Annie's just been giving me my orders," I said.

Captain Prosser gave a bark of laughter. "I bet she has!" he said. "I've served under admirals who frightened me less than our Annie." Sometimes he overdoes the bluff seafarer.

"Isn't she marvelous," Judith said. "All the things she does for the village — I can't imagine what we'd do without her. And always full of new schemes, like the Book — such a marvelous idea, and, of course, she has all those wonderful family photos and things going way back!"

"There certainly seems to be a lot of material," I said without enthusiasm. I turned to Diana. "I believe Toby has quite a few things that we might include."

"There's a lot of junk out in the barn if the rats haven't got to it," she said carelessly. "A couple of old trunks full of God knows what. You're welcome to have a look at it if you like."

"It's very kind of you," I said hastily, "but I'm sure Annie would rather look through things herself — she is in overall charge. I'm just doing the background stuff: the history of the village itself, documents in the County Records Office, things like that."

"Documents, how *interesting*," Judith said reverently. "As well as all the things from people in the village — people from every walk of life. The rich man in his castle, the poor man at the gate, as you might say."

There was a slightly uneasy silence at this politically incorrect statement.

"Did you know," I said hastily, "that Mrs. Alexander wrote that hymn when she was staying down here at Dunster? I believe the purple-headed mountain was Grabbist and the river running by was the Avill."

Diana raised an eyebrow. "Fascinating," she said.

"Of course, you'd know all about that sort of thing," Mary Fletcher said, "since you're such an expert on the Victorians."

"I'd hardly say that," I protested.

"When I was working in the library at Farnborough," she went on, "I found your books were quite popular — for books of that sort, of course."

"Really," I said weakly, "how interesting."

"Well," Judith said, "what with your books and Father William's broadcasts we have two celebrities in the village! Oh, and Mr. Parker, of course." She turned to Diana. "It's a great privilege to have a real live Member of Parliament right here on our doorstep!"

"I must remember," Diana said, "to tell Toby that he is real and alive."

Judith gave her an uncertain smile. "Anyway," she said, "I know we're all looking forward to this book."

"I hope you can get it out soon," Captain Prosser said. "Quite a few villages have already published theirs — I've seen them in Smith's — and we don't want to be seen lagging behind."

"These things can't be rushed; there's a great deal involved in publishing a book, you know," Mary said, with the confident air of one who had professional knowledge of such matters. "Even today with the new technology."

"Oh, *that*," the captain said. "I can't make heads or tails of it. Wouldn't have one of those computers if you gave it to me!"

"I took a very good course when I was at Farnborough," Mary said. "It was quite advanced — well, you had to be right up-to-date in the library — but I believe there are several really simple ones for beginners."

While this exchange was going on I'd edged my way to the counter and addressed Maurice Sanders, who'd been listening to his customers' conversation in an abstracted way.

"What I really came in for," I said, "is some of that delicious smoked eel pâté you have."

"I'm so sorry." He shook his head. "It's

very popular — goes almost as soon as I get it in. But I'm expecting some next Tuesday. I'll put some by for you."

"Thank you so much," I said. "I'll look forward to that. I expect I'll be back and forth to the village quite a bit now."

And whether that would be a good thing I couldn't, at the moment, decide.

CHAPTER THREE

"How are you settling in?" Rosemary asked as we sat at one of the small, unsteady tables in the Buttery.

"It was strange at first," Rachel said, "being back in my childhood home. And Phyll's put me in my old room, which feels a bit weird — it feels as though time has telescoped."

"I'm sure she's delighted to have you back," I said. "She's seemed really lost since your father died."

"It was marvelous, the way she looked after him. There wasn't much I could do to help, being so far away, and then, of course, there was Alastair's long illness . . ." Her voice trailed away.

"That must have been awful for you," Rosemary said, "and with Jamie abroad. Africa, isn't it?"

"Somalia. He's working in one of those terrible refugee camps."

"It's splendid," I said, "the work he's doing. I mean, he's so highly qualified — to give all that up to go and help out there."

"It's what he wanted to do," Rachel said. "Alastair was disappointed at first. He hoped Jamie would take over the practice, but then, when he saw how serious he was, he gave him a lot of support. I miss them both so much and, of course, I worry about Jamie a lot. So," she said briskly, "this move back here is a good thing — there's been so much to do, which helps keep my mind off things."

"I expect it feels strange, sharing a house," Rosemary said.

"The trouble is the kitchen — well, you know how you feel about your own kitchen. The fact is, both Phyll and I love to cook. She's brilliant and I'm not bad, though I'm not in her league."

"Oh dear. So what are you going to do?"

"The only thing we can do — we've made a sort of roster: I cook on Monday, Wednesday and Friday and Phyll has Tuesday, Thursday and Saturday. Sundays we take turns. We each shop for our own days and we each do our own washing up."

"It *sounds* all right," Rosemary said. "How's it working so far?"

"Not bad, really. Of course it's very difficult getting used to other people's stove, saucepans and so forth, but I'm working on it."

"Well-done, both of you," I said.

"Oh, Phyll tries so hard to make things easy, bless her, and of course, we have Mrs. Bradshaw twice a week to do the housework and so forth, which helps a lot. Fortunately we're both naturally tidy — Mother saw to that!"

Remembering Mrs. Gregory, I could well believe it. She was a highly intelligent woman who had the misfortune to live at a time when it was unusual for a married woman to have a career, so she put her energies into being the perfect doctor's wife. She would, of course, have liked her husband to achieve the higher reaches of his profession, but dear Dr. Gregory, although immensely easygoing, refused point-blank to be anything other than a respected (and much loved) GP, practicing in Taviscombe and living in the house he adored at Mere Barton. Being a realist, Margaret Gregory accepted this, and devoted herself to (unobtrusively) helping her husband in his practice, organizing his social life and running every voluntary organization in the district. Since she felt that the family picture required children, she had two. She was deeply disappointed when her second child was another girl (she had reckoned on one of each), but deciding that girls were easier to mold than boys (of whom she had no personal knowledge and whom she regarded with a certain degree of distaste), she determined that Rachel and Phyllis should be perfect in every respect. And I'm sure that included tidiness.

"We go our separate ways to some extent," Rachel went on. "Phyll has quite a few commitments in the village and I'm still trying to adjust to things down here."

"I'm sure," Rosemary said, "there'll be lots of places that would be glad of your help. Brunswick Lodge," she suggested, "for one."

"Is Anthea still running things?"

Rosemary nodded.

"Then I certainly won't get involved *there*, just as I'm steering clear of all Annie Roberts's things in the village."

"There's the Hospital Friends," I suggested. "They're a nice bunch, and with your nurse's training you could bring a bit of practical common sense to some of the discussions!"

Rachel smiled. "I don't think I'll commit myself to anything for a while. I just want to keep my head down and find my feet. Is that a mixed metaphor? Anyway, you know what I mean. I'm still getting used to the changes in the village; nearly half the people have come since I was here last. Phyll seems to like most of them, but I can't help resenting them as interlopers! Thank heaven for dear old Ellen; we occasionally get together and have a really good grumble."

"Yes," I said, "she was being very forthright about things when I saw her yesterday. I had to see Annie about this wretched village book she's forcing me to help with, and Ellen very kindly rescued me from what could have been a *very* long session!"

"Oh yes, I heard about this famous book," Rachel said. "It's ranked second after the Domesday Book, in Annie's opinion."

"Oh, don't mention the Domesday Book!" I exclaimed. "She's making me spend hours in the County Records Office looking up ancient documents. She's set her heart on proving that Mere Barton is *older* than any of the other villages. Apparently it's a matter of pride!"

Rachel laughed. "Mere Barton forever! But that's enough about the village. What I really want to hear is all the news about both of you. Hang on a minute; I'm going to get us all fresh coffees and some Danish pastries. Yes," she added as we made token protests, "don't argue — after all, this is a sort of celebration."

"So, what's all this I hear about you getting mixed up with one of Annie Roberts's projects?" Michael asked when I was having a family lunch with them the following Sunday. "I hope you know what you're letting yourself in for."

"I'm beginning to," I said.

"What exactly are you doing?" Thea asked.

"Oh, I'm supposed to be helping with this book about Mere Barton — well, I say helping, but it seems to me that Annie's shifting most of the work onto me."

Michael laughed. "Typical! She comes up with these schemes and off-loads the actual work onto other people and then, when they're finished, she takes all the credit for them herself."

"Ellen Tucker says she can be an absolute monster sometimes," I said.

My granddaughter, who had been pushing the mashed potato round her plate in a desultory fashion, looked up with interest. "A monster?" she asked. "Like a tyrannosaurus?"

"No, darling," I said. "It's just a figure of speech."

"What's a figure —"

"Alice," said her father, "stop being a pain! Eat up your food and stop playing with it." He turned to me. "No, I've had some very tiresome dealings with Miss Roberts."

"Really?"

"It's one of these wretched charitable trusts. Many, many years ago a Miss Percy, who was the sister of the rector of Mere Barton at the time, left a sum of money in trust for the poor of the village."

"That was nice," Thea said.

"I wouldn't say there were any poor in Mere Barton these days!" I said.

"She also," Michael went on, ignoring our interruptions, "left a piece of land to be used in common by all the villagers to graze their animals."

"Whereabouts is it?" I asked.

"About half a mile outside the village proper — well, so many new houses have been built there that now it's almost *in* the village."

"Well, apart from Diana and her horses," I said, "I can't think of anyone who'd want to graze anything there nowadays. Anyway, Diana's got a perfectly good paddock and she's not what you'd call *poor*."

"Exactly. So we — that is, most of the trustees, feel it's time to wind up the trust."

"So?"

"So Annie Roberts doesn't agree."

"How come Annie's one of the trustees?"

"The bequest specifies that one of them has to be a resident of the village and —"

"And Annie snaffled the job!"

"Precisely."

"Is she the only one who objects?"

"Well, there is one other — Brian Norris — who seems to object to things on principle."

"Oh, I know him from the Hospital Friends."

"But I'm pretty sure he could be persuaded. No, it's Annie who's the problem."

"But surely you could all outvote her."

"Unfortunately we can't. All decisions have to be unanimous."

"How awkward," I said. "What do you want to do with the land?"

"Actually, we've had a very good offer for it from someone who wants to build houses there. It's a couple of acres and you could get quite a few houses on that, even large expensive ones like the rest of the ones in Mere Barton."

"What about planning permission?"

"There've been so many new houses built there in the last ten years without any problem, so I don't think that will be a difficulty."

"Yes, well, I sort of see Annie's point — still more houses . . ."

"I agree," Thea said, getting up to remove the plates and fetch the pudding. "The village is quite built up enough already."

"Anyway," I said, "what would happen to all this money if you do sell?"

"It goes to the charity commissioners."

"You mean you just have to hand it over?"

"That's right — cy pres, if you want the legal term. I think it's Norman French."

"And what do they do with it?"

"They pass it on to some other charity."

"So it's not kept in the village?"

"No."

"Well," I said, "I must say I agree with Annie. After all, Miss Thingummy, who set up the trust, expected it would stay in the village."

"It doesn't work like that — it's the law."

"The law is an ass."

"True, but there it is."

"So the only people who'll do well out of the whole affair will be these property developers."

"They will, yes, but other charities will benefit."

"And this sort of thing's going on all over the country?"

"Well . . . yes, I suppose it is. That kind of

benefaction — soup and blankets for the poor — doesn't work anymore."

"No, I suppose not," I said sadly, "and although the poor are still with us (and in villages too), I expect they'd feel patronized by Victorian charities whereas they can accept state aid quite happily. And a good thing too. It's just sentimental to want that sort of old custom to survive."

Thea's return to the dining room bearing a splendid trifle put an end to this discussion, but I retained my sense of dissatisfaction about the affair and when I saw Rosemary the next day I asked her if she knew about it.

"I seem to remember Jack had something to do with the money side of a charity at Old Cleeve. I suppose they have to do something — I mean, you can't just leave it lying idle forever."

"No, but there must be things in the village it could be used for. The church usually needs money for restoring *something,* and if this benefactor was a former Rector's sister, I bet that's what she'd have wanted."

"Well, yes . . ."

I laughed. "Just for once I'm on Annie's side."

"Do you think she'll go on holding things up?"

"Oh yes, there's no way she'll give in."

"I wonder what everyone else in the village thinks."

"A lot of them wouldn't like more new houses in the village."

"But most of them live in new houses."

"Exactly. But then, *they* want to preserve their rural idyll. I expect Maurice Sanders would welcome more trade for the village shop and Father William would like a larger congregation — if they're churchgoers."

"It's amazing what Annie gets done," Rosemary said, "even if she uses other people to do it."

"I just wish I knew how she does it — use other people, I mean. *I* usually end up being one of the other people, especially if it's someone like Annie or Anthea doing the using."

"I was amused at Rachel saying she's steering clear of Anthea and Annie — I bet she won't be able to help herself."

"Well, she seems to have used all her organizing skills over the kitchen problem."

"I'm not sure about that," Rosemary said doubtfully. "I can't see it lasting — Rachel won't be able to help herself taking over — just you wait and see!"

"She always was very much the elder sister, not just being bossy, but protective too. Do you remember when Zoe Havisham tried to bully Phyll, how Rachel put the fear of God into her?"

"Goodness, yes. I'd forgotten all about Zoe; she was a nasty piece of work. She left the following year, didn't she? I wonder what happened to her."

"Oh, her parents had split up — I expect she was unhappy and that's why she was so beastly — and her mother married again and they all moved up to Newcastle."

"Really?" Rosemary said in surprise. "I suppose that would explain it. How do you know these things?"

I shrugged. "I just do. I suppose I hear someone talking about things and they sort of seep into my subconscious."

"Anyway," Rosemary said, "whatever her good intentions, I bet Rachel will take over and I daresay Phyll will let her — that's what they've always done."

"Even though they've led separate lives all these years?"

"Oh, I think so."

"I don't know how it would be with a sister," I said thoughtfully. "It's different with a brother, and Jeremy was a lot older than me — as Colin was with you — so there was never any question of who stood where in the hierarchy."

"That's true. And in their case it wasn't really about who was the older — there was only just over a year between them. But Rachel's always been a much stronger character than Phyll and she'd have taken the lead anyway."

I thought about this when I met Phyll in the chemist a few days later.

"How's everything going?" I asked.

"Oh, it's fine," she said. "It's almost as though Rachel's never been away."

"Rachel told us about the kitchen roster," I said tentatively. "Is it working out all right?"

She laughed. "Well, it needs a bit of give-and-take and I suppose I do most of the giving. But it must be very difficult for Rache, after all those years of running her own home, and I don't mind if it makes her happy. No, we're settling in really well and it's lovely to have her here." She paused for a moment and said, "I was very down after Father died. I missed him so much. People in the village were kind and sympathetic, but I felt very alone. Friends are all very well, but there's nothing like your own family — so now it's perfect."

As I drove home I thought how fortunate it was that Phyll had such an affectionate and accommodating nature. Perhaps we'd been too pessimistic and things would work out happily after all.

CHAPTER FOUR

After putting it off and finding many plausible reasons for not doing anything about it, I decided I really must get down to the research I had to do for the Book. As a way of easing myself into it gently, I rang Father William and asked if I could come and look at the church records.

"Oh, do," he said enthusiastically. "Come over right away. Tuesday is always such a dismal day, don't you think? It will be so cheering to have a nice chat."

The rectory at Mere Barton, a fine early Victorian building, has long since been secularized and sold off (to a film producer who lives in it for only a few months of the year), so Father William now lives in a new bungalow built on what used to be the vegetable garden of the old house.

He greeted me effusively and ushered me into a large room with bookshelves covering every wall.

"Do come into the study," he said. "I'm tempted to call it the library, but that would be too pretentious, don't you think?"

"It's a charming room," I said. And, indeed, it was. The bookshelves were painted white so the general effect wasn't at all oppressive. Indeed, the brightly colored jackets on some of the books (no solemn leather-bound sermons here) gave the room a positively lively feel. There were a couple of armchairs and several small antique tables and, facing the window, a handsome mahogany desk with an expensive reading lamp. A large flower arrangement stood on a Pembroke table and there was a screen worked in gros point in the empty hearth of a proper fireplace. Over the fireplace hung a large oil painting of a gentleman in eighteenth-century dress leaning elegantly against a column in a formal landscape, and I wondered if he was an ancestor or merely "bought-in."

"How sweet of you to say so. One does one's best, but it's hard to achieve any sort of elegance in a *bungalow*." His voice sharpened as he pronounced the word. "How one regrets the old rectory — such vandalism!"

"It does seem a shame," I said.

"I was tempted by the vicarage at Higher Barton," he said. "You know I have three

54

parishes (so exhausting), but it was appalling. The former incumbent lived there and he had four children (imagine!). So, of course, everything was in a dreadful state. And the church commissioners refused to do more than the absolute *minimum,* so it was quite impossible. Besides, Mere Barton is quite the most sympathetic of the three villages."

I didn't know the two other villages in question and wondered idly what special qualities in Mere Barton and its inhabitants he found so sympathetic.

"Well," I said brightly, "I'm sure everyone is delighted that you chose to live here, even if it is," I added unkindly, "in a bungalow."

"I know — that was unworthy, wasn't it. But I do feel it's easier to live a good life in pleasant surroundings."

"What does Gilbert say in *Iolanthe?* 'Hearts just as true and fair/May live in Belgrave Square/As in the lowly air of Seven Dials.' "

He gave me one of his charming smiles. "Now you're laughing at me, and quite right too. But it would be so nice to have been one of those clergymen like Kilvert or Parson Woodford (all that lovely food!) or Sidney Smith — just down the road at Combe Florey — writing splendid letters or keeping a wonderful literary journal."

"Well," I said, "you have your radio talks. I suppose that's the modern equivalent."

"Oh, do you think so? What a delightful thought. And I suppose I do take a lot of my material from the village, as they did. But, dear me, what must you think of me, chattering away — I'll just go and get the coffee."

He went out of the room and I took the opportunity of going over to examine a photograph on the narrow mantelpiece above the fireplace. It was of a strikingly handsome man in army uniform — I thought a colonel, but I'm never sure about crowns and things. He looked very stern and unbending and his piercing gaze seemed to accuse me of prying, so I averted my eyes and was innocently admiring the eighteenth-century gentleman in his rural setting when Father William returned with a tray.

"What a splendid picture," I said. "He looks very grand. I love his waistcoat, such a lovely color and all that gorgeous embroidery."

"Very becoming, but I wouldn't fancy the wig; I believe they quickly became very unsanitary." So not an ancestor, then, since I was sure he would certainly have told me if it was. He put the tray on the desk and continued. "Do sit down, and I'll pour the coffee. There are some of Phyllis's delicious shortbread biscuits that she kindly brought for me the other day."

"How lovely. She's a marvelous cook, and Rachel's very good too. I gather they've divided the domestic duties between them."

"Yes, Rachel has settled nicely and they do seem to get on very well — *not* always the case where relatives are concerned."

I wondered whether the stern military figure was a relative.

"Oh, they've always been very devoted," I said, "ever since they were children."

"Of course, you were all at school together — how I envy you that. I never seemed to stay in one school long enough to make any friends — a sort of peripatetic life."

"Really?" I said inquiringly, hoping for some sort of personal history, but he put a cup of coffee on the little table beside me and changed the subject.

"So, you're going to be writing this splendid book," he said.

"Not actually writing it," I said hastily. "Just helping Annie with some of the research."

"Don't you believe it — once Annie's got you involved you'll be doing more than just helping. Annie's absolutely brilliant at *organizing.* Need I say more?"

"Oh dear." I sighed. "That's what everyone says. I really can't spare the time to do the whole thing."

"Well" — he looked at me quizzically — "if you feel up to telling Annie that . . ."

I laughed reluctantly. "I see what you mean. Oh well, I'll just have to do the best I can. So what about the church records?"

"Ah well, most of the important ones — the really old, historical ones — have gone to the County Records Office, but you are very welcome to see what we still have. Most churches have given up their parish registers and only have photocopies, but I felt it was important to keep ours in the village — something tangible, as it were, for the villagers to see and handle if they wished. Meanwhile" — he got to his feet and went over to the desk and took something out of one of the drawers — "you may conceivably find something useful in this." He handed me an elegantly printed little booklet. "It's a short history of the church. A poor thing but mine own."

"But this is absolutely splendid," I said, turning the pages. "Lovely old engravings too. Goodness, it must have been very expensive to produce something like this!"

"Well," he said, "it was rather beyond the means of the parish council."

"So you paid for it yourself?"

He shrugged. "Having spent some time on it, I felt it deserved a slightly better presentation than a photocopied typescript. And we do have quite a few visitors — people who rather want to see the church I've mentioned in my broadcasts." He smiled the charming smile again. "Such is the result of even minor media attention. But you will know all about that — your splendid radio talk about Mrs. Gaskell must, I'm sure, have reached a wide audience."

He inclined his head slightly, as if to include me in that small circle of "celebrities."

I put my coffee cup down on the table and got to my feet. "Well, if you have a moment, perhaps we could go up to the church and have a look at the records you have there."

As we walked through the churchyard he pointed out things of interest — the ancient yew tree, the remains of the old preaching cross, a gravestone recording that, in 1865, Joshua Minns died from a wall falling on him. As I watched his tall, cassocked figure moving among the graves, I felt how absolutely right such a figure looks in such a place.

The church struck chill. "No heating except for services," he said. "Strict economy is our rule — *faute de mieux,* I'm afraid."

"It seems suitable somehow," I said, "that the inside of a church should be a different temperature from the world outside." I instinctively lowered my voice, not being, like Trollope's Lily Dale, one accustomed to speaking conversationally in church.

"No tombs," he said regretfully. "No recumbent Elizabethan figures surrounded by kneeling deceased children. Still, we do have a remarkably fine screen and the font is fifteenth century."

He led the way into the vestry, unlocked a cupboard and produced some parish registers, saying, "I think these will be the most useful things I can provide. They go back a fair way."

I opened one of the heavy volumes and glanced through the pages.

"These will be splendid, but I think I'd like to come and spend some time looking at them properly and making notes."

He nodded. "Of course; just let me know when. Oh, and do bring your laptop if you want to — we welcome the new technology!"

I left him in the vestry and made my way out of the church. As I was going towards the rectory to collect my car, I was hailed from behind. It was Annie Roberts.

"Oh, Sheila, just the person — can you just pop in and have a look at some old letters I think you really ought to include?"

"Oh, well . . ." I began.

"It won't take a moment."

Obviously it was impossible to refuse, so I followed her up the village street and into her cottage.

"Do you always leave your door unlocked?" I asked curiously.

"Why wouldn't I?"

"Well, is it safe?"

She laughed. "I was only going up to the shop," she said, "and there's always someone about in the street. It's not like in a town, now, is it?"

We went into her sitting room and she sat me down at the large round table and laid several bundles of letters before me.

"I saw you going into the rectory earlier," she said, "so I reckoned you'd be up at the church sometime. Looking at the parish registers, were you? Well now, see what you think of these. They're letters I found in an old suitcase of my mother's — a lot of stuff there. These are ones my grandfather wrote

61

when he was in France in the First World War. Now, what do you say about that?"

I picked up one of the bundles and touched it gently. The paper was stiff and brown at the edges, the ink faded.

It was, somehow, a very emotional moment, and I suddenly felt I couldn't examine them with Annie's eyes upon me.

"I wonder," I said, "would you mind if I took them away and had photocopies made so that I can work on them at home? Then I can return the originals; they must be very precious to you."

She seemed disconcerted and I wondered if she'd expected us to read them together, something I didn't think I could bear to do.

"Well, yes, I suppose . . ." she began.

"I'll take great care of them," I said, "and let you have them back in a few days. If you have a bag or something I could put them in?"

"I think so. Come into the kitchen and I'll see what I can find."

I followed her along the narrow hallway into a surprisingly roomy kitchen with a stone sink and an old Aga range (both original, not part of a trendy makeover), high cupboards all round and a large table taking up most of the space in the middle. Annie had obviously been preparing a meal;

there was a wooden board with chopped-up carrots and onions, a pot half filled with meat and a basket of mushrooms. Though, when I looked more closely, they weren't mushrooms, but a variety of fungi.

"Good gracious," I said, picking up the basket, "are you going to cook with these? Aren't they dangerous?"

She looked up from the drawer in the table where she'd been looking for a bag and laughed.

"Dangerous? Bless you, no! Not if you know what you're doing. We've always used them — much better than field mushrooms, more flavor. My mother, now, she was a proper countrywoman. She taught us all about things like that — not just these, but herbs and remedies. They used to say in the village she was better than any doctor and, before the war, cheaper too!"

"Do you ever make up remedies?" I asked.

"Well, no, it wouldn't have been proper, seeing as I was a health service practitioner, as you might say. Though I suppose it's what you'd call alternative medicine now — better than some of that stuff you get in health shops. But I do occasionally make up something for colds and suchlike, just for myself and people who ask me."

"How splendid," I said. "I'll know where

to come next time I have a cold!"

"I always said," Rosemary declared, when I told her about it, "that Annie is a witch."

"A sort of wise woman," I suggested.

"Well, I don't know about wise. But fancy all that going on at Mere Barton nowadays! Are you going to put it in the Book?"

I smiled. "I don't think so. I fancy Annie — although she's quite proud of her peculiar talents — doesn't really want them publicized."

"I wonder if that's how she makes people do what she wants?" Rosemary said. "Perhaps she casts spells over them."

"You never know."

"Anyway," Rosemary went on, "how about Father William? What's his house like?"

"Bungalow — as he is quick to inform one, with some distaste. Apparently he feels he should be living in more dignified surroundings. Though I must say he's done his best to create a splendidly elegant ambience. He has what you might call beautiful *things* — pictures, objets and so forth."

"Goodness!"

"I sometimes wonder," I said thoughtfully, "what he's really like underneath that affected manner."

"About the same, I should think."

"Maybe. He gave me a copy of a booklet he's written about the church, and it's a really scholarly piece of work. He's obviously put a lot of thought and research into it."

"Oh well," Rosemary said, "I suppose you can be affected and a scholar as well; look at all those television arts presenters!"

When I put the phone down I found the booklet and looked at it again. As well as meticulous research there was a real feeling of involvement, and I suddenly thought of how he must have stood many times looking at the list of rectors on the board in the church porch and thinking of all those past incumbents from 1292 (when the living was valued at seven marks, three shillings and four pence) down to himself in the present day.

As I was cutting up some mushrooms to go in the omelette I was making for supper, and thinking about Annie's expertise with fungi, the phone rang. It was Rachel asking if Rosemary and I would like to go with them to the Mere Barton Harvest Supper the following week.

"Do come," she said. "We're each of us allowed to bring a guest. It's quite fun really and the food is always good. Everyone in the village contributes something — Phyll's been in the kitchen for days now, cooking up little delicacies. I can't really compete, but I've done a few boring things like quiches and sausage rolls."

"I'd love to come," I said, "and I'm sure Rosemary would too."

"Oh, good. Anyway, what with the Book and everything, you're practically part of the village yourself."

"Does that mean I should contribute something too?"

"No, no, you and Rosemary are guests, though I do have happy memories of your lemon drizzle cake and I know that would go down very well!"

As I went back to my omelette I smiled when I thought about how well Rachel seemed to be settling down and taking part in village life. I wondered if she could resist trying to take over some of Annie's activities and, if she did, what Annie would do about that.

CHAPTER FIVE

The village hall looked very nice. There were proper tablecloths on the trestle tables and arrangements of autumn leaves and flowers at intervals along them. A buffet was laid out at one end of the hall with a wonderful display of food and, I was pleased to see, bottles of wine and glasses.

"Goodness," Rosemary said, gesturing towards a large ham and a whole salmon with a carapace of thin slices of cucumber, "how very fancy!"

Rachel, who had been talking to Mary Fletcher, came over to greet us, and I handed her my cake.

"A modest contribution," I said, "to what looks like a very elegant feast!"

"And a little something from me," Rosemary said, giving her two bottles, "on the principle that you can't have too much drink on such occasions."

"Oh, bless you both. How kind. Now, do

come and mingle; most people are here now. I'll just go and give these to Annie, who, you won't be surprised to learn, is busily organizing people in the kitchen."

"Rosemary and Sheila, how lovely to see you!" Toby Parker was approaching us, both hands outstretched in greeting. His charming smile was a little different from Father William's, being more personal and less universal — the difference, perhaps, between the temporal and the spiritual. "Ages since I saw you both." He turned to Rosemary. "How's Jack? Still number crunching?" To me he said, "And that clever son of yours, Sheila — has he been tempted away to some high-powered legal practice in London? Quite right — London's a terrible place to be now, so exhausting. I just wish I could live down here always like Diana, sensible girl, and be a country gent and ride to hounds!"

I noticed that "exhausting" was the word that sprang readily to mind in the representatives of both church and state.

"It must be horrid," I said. "Though, if it gets too much for you, you could always retire."

He laughed politely. "I might just do that. But I simply couldn't resist coming down for the Harvest Supper. Such happy memories of it in the old days — quite different now, of course. When I was a boy it was the event of the year — all the workers on the farm and their wives and children, in the big barn; a real knees-up. Well, you can imagine — all that home-brewed cider!"

"I imagine this will be a more formal affair," I said.

"Is Diana coming?" Rosemary asked.

"Something the matter with one of the horses, but she hopes to be along later."

"Are you down here for long?" I asked, not that I particularly wanted to know, but somehow I always found myself making this kind of all-purpose conversation with Toby, probably because I only ever seemed to see his public face, and what else could one say to that?

"Only for a few days, I'm afraid. There's a rather important parliamentary committee that I'm sitting on — public transport, very boring — and I have to be back for that, but I do hope to have a little time down here before the House sits again."

I could sense, rather than hear, Rosemary give a little sardonic snort at this and I hastened to say, "They do seem to have put on a wonderful spread — all that marvelous food and drink. And I believe Marcus Hardy — you know, he lives at Lark Hill, just outside the village — bought an old cider press last year, so we may even have home-brewed cider!"

"Ah, but it won't be like the old stuff. I can remember as a boy sitting with the men in the cider house passing round an enormous jar, and the cider was really rough and had bits of goodness knows what floating around in it and you had to drink it or else you'd lose face!"

"Telling you about the old days on the farm, is he?" Annie had joined us. She turned to Toby. "Thought you were saving all those stories for when you come to write your memoirs — that's what you politicians do, isn't it, when you give up? Make a bit of money selling it to the Sunday papers."

He gave her the MP smile, a little uneasily, I thought. "Oh, I've got a great deal of material," he said, "political and otherwise, but I do have a special feeling for this part of the world; after all, as I was saying just now, I'm a countryman at heart."

"I suppose that's why," Annie said sharply, "you have a London constituency."

The smile again. "Ah, we politicians have to take what we can get."

"The best of both worlds," I said, feeling obliged to break up what seemed like a tense moment. "Aren't you lucky!"

"Oh, I wouldn't want to live in London," Rosemary said. "I did when I was young. I thought it would be lovely to live where the really important things were happening. But now everything's changed and changed for the worse."

"Oh, I wouldn't say that," Toby said. "London's still an exciting place to be, though, of course, I'm fortunate to be at the center of things, as it were."

"None of you lot are ever there," Annie said. "When I watch that Parliament channel on my Sky TV — I like to keep up — the place is always half empty. No, not even that, just someone speaking and one or two people round him, and then a lot of empty seats. I don't call that a job of work!"

"A lot of the work is done in committee," Toby said, with an air of controlled patience. "As I was explaining earlier, I'm serving on a rather important one, on public transport . . ."

"Will it give us a better bus service to Bridgwater?" Annie demanded. "No, I didn't think so. Well, I can't stand here chatting; I've got to get back and see what they're up to in the kitchen."

"Well," Rosemary said when Annie had gone, "she doesn't mince her words, does she?"

Toby laughed. "Oh, Annie and I understand each other; we more or less grew up together. In fact, I do believe that, apart from Fred and Ellen Tucker, we are the last original inhabitants still living in the village."

"The last of the aboriginals," I said. "Ellen was talking about it just the other day."

"Of course," Toby said, "rural depopulation is a serious matter. I hope to bring a private Member's Bill on that very subject."

Since Toby was now embarked on what appeared to be a rerun of one of his parliamentary speeches, I was relieved when Rachel came up.

"Oh, Toby, sorry to interrupt, but everything's ready now, so if you could gather people together and say a few words. Just introduce the entertainment — they're all ready — and then after that Father William will say a prayer and we'll all get on with the eating and drinking, which is the main thing, really!"

Certainly the food was marvelous. When the entertainment was over Rosemary and I, who'd been getting hungrier by the minute, filled our plates (rather greedily) and sat down at one of the tables. We'd just settled when we were joined by Jim and Mary Fletcher — not the people I would have chosen to spend the evening with, but they chatted amiably enough about the food and the entertainment we were promised.

"Weren't those handbell ringers from Lower Barton wonderful?" Jim said. "They're really quite remarkable."

"Such an old tradition," Mary said. "And of course we have a very fine peal in the church here; I expect you've heard them. In the olden days they used to muffle the bells on New Year's Eve to alternate the six normal rings for the New Year with six almost inaudible for the old. Isn't that interesting — perhaps you could put it in the Book."

"How fascinating," I said, with what conviction I could muster.

"Oh, Mary will put you right," Jim said. "Very interested in things like that — always has been. When we were living in Farnborough she was very involved with the local history society. Working in the library, you see, she was able to look up all sorts of things for them. I'm sure she could do the same for you here — she's struck up quite a friendship with the chief librarian in Taviscombe, haven't you, Mary?"

"Well, of course I'd be only too glad to do what I can to help," Mary said stiffly. "I understood that Annie was going to compile it all herself and I thought she might have been glad of a little assistance, since she's always so busy. But, of course, I do see that a proper author, like Sheila here, would be the person to ask."

"I must say I thought Annie was doing it all," I said, recognizing umbrage when I heard it. "But apparently she expects me to do more or less the whole thing, which I really hadn't bargained for. So I'd certainly be *most* grateful if you could spare the time — there's a great deal to do and I'm sure, with your experience, you'd be exactly the right person."

"There you are, Mary," Jim said. "I told you Sheila would appreciate your help. Why don't you come round one morning, Sheila, to have some coffee and a chat?"

"That would be lovely," I said. "Do give me a ring and we'll arrange a date. Now," I continued, standing up, "I think I must just have a tiny slice of that delicious chocolate cake while there's still some left. How about you, Rosemary?"

"Oh dear," Rosemary said when we were out of earshot, "do you really want to work with Mary Fletcher?"

"To be honest," I said, "I'll be delighted to work with anyone who's willing to take some of the burden — there really is so much to do and I know Annie will be badgering me if I'm not doing things quickly enough for her. No, I'll be glad to off-load as much as she'll take!"

Diana, underdressed, I thought, for such an occasion in jeans, shirt and a body warmer, was pouring herself a glass of red wine at the buffet. She held up the bottle and looked at the label. "Australian merlot," she said. "I suppose it could be worse."

"Oh, Australian wines are splendid," I said, "almost my favorites." Diana gave the impression of raising her eyebrows without actually doing so. "Though, of course," I added, "I usually drink only one solitary glass of wine with my supper."

It's odd, really, the way I always make fatuous remarks when talking to Diana. Rosemary says it's a sort of disdain on my part, not thinking her worthy of a rational reply.

"How's the horse?" Rosemary asked. "Toby said one of them wasn't well."

"Caught his leg on some wire when we were out last Tuesday," Diana said briefly, "so I've got to put fomentations on it."

"Oh dear," I said, "that's quite a business."

"A blessing tonight." She laughed. "That way I didn't have to sit through the ghastly 'entertainment' — last year it was those dreary handbell ringers and that grisly woman singing folk songs, or some old man telling endless dialect stories."

"Well, there's still quite lot of food left," I said helpfully. "It's very good."

"I don't really want anything," she said. "I'll just have a bit of quiche and some of this *wilted* salad. Oh, and another drink." She drained her glass, refilled it and drank again. "Did Toby say his piece like a good little MP?" I wondered just how much she'd had to drink before she arrived. "And I suppose dear Father William said grace, or whatever you call it — God, that man is so camp — no wonder he wanders around all the time in that frock! And all this broadcasting nonsense, so ridiculous!" She put some food on her plate with an unsteady hand so that some of the salad spilled onto the cloth. She laughed again, rather more loudly. "Oh dear, mustn't make a mess, or that old bat Annie Roberts will never let me hear the last of it." She picked the salad carefully off the cloth and put it on her plate. "There, now." She lowered her voice and leaned confidentially towards us. "Now she'll never know! Thinks she knows everything — she's a witch."

"Won't you sit down," Rosemary said.

"It's so much easier to manage a plate and a glass." She led Diana away to an empty table and gave me a speaking look. Interpreting it correctly, I looked around for Toby. He was listening somewhat abstractedly to Captain Prosser and seemed relieved when I drew him away.

"I think Diana is a little unwell," I said. "Perhaps she should go home."

"Oh God, not again! I don't know what's got into her these days; she never used to get into this state." He looked across to where Rosemary was urging Diana to eat some of her quiche. "Oh well, I've done my bit here, so I suppose I'd better take her home before it becomes too obvious. Thank God she didn't drive down here. Bless you, Sheila."

Their departure seemed somehow a signal for other people to go.

"I think we might get away now," Rosemary said. "We ought to find Rachel and Phyll and thank them."

"Rachel and Phyllis?" Ellen said when we asked. "I think they're in the kitchen."

The kitchen, like the rest of the village hall, reflected the prosperity of the village. There was a large catering-style cooker with two ovens, as well as a microwave, a big refrigerator, a dishwasher, a gleaming double sink, ample cupboards and fitted work tops all round. Phyll was unloading the dishwasher while Rachel and Judith Lamb were helping Annie sort out the remains of the food.

"Not a lot left," Judith said.

"I'm not surprised," I said. "It was gorgeous."

"I've got a couple of boxes here," Rachel said to Annie. "Shall I pack some stuff for each of you? It seems such a shame to waste it."

"I'd be glad of some of it," Judith said. "Save me cooking for lunch and supper tomorrow. How about you, Annie?"

"I hate seeing good food go to waste — I don't mind using it up. This green stuff will have to go out — thought at the time you were making too much, Rachel — and the fruit salad. It's always a mistake to put bananas in a fruit salad; they only go brown. Pass me the rubbish bag, Judith, but don't put it out tonight or the foxes will tear it open. There should be a collection tomorrow, but you never know with this council — useless lot!"

I turned to Rachel. "We just wanted to say good-bye and thank you so much for inviting us; it was a lovely evening."

"Lovely," Rosemary said, "and heavenly

food. I'll give you a ring and we'll get together soon."

Annie looked up from tying up the bin bag. "Don't forget, Sheila, I need to go over those letters with you sometime soon — there's a lot to do."

"Yes, of course," I said. "I'll get the photocopies done so I can start reading them; then I can return the originals to you. Anyway, Mary Fletcher said she'd be willing to help — looking things up and so forth."

"That woman — she won't be much use to you. Thinks too much of herself." She gave the string round the bag a vicious tug. "Thought *she* was going to do it all. Just because she used to work in a library. I soon put her straight about that!"

"I'm sure she'll be a help in checking things, dates and things like that," I said placatingly.

"Well, don't blame me if she makes a mess of things," she said, seizing a cloth and vigorously wiping down the work top.

"Well," Rosemary said, edging toward the door, "it's been a wonderful evening; we've enjoyed it so much."

In the car going home Rosemary said, "What on earth got into Diana? Not like her to make an exhibition of herself on a couple of glasses of wine."

"I rather think she'd been drinking before she came — she obviously hadn't bothered to change after seeing to her horse. But I wouldn't have thought she was the sort of person who'd hit the bottle. I wonder what's wrong."

"Being married to that clown Toby?"

"She's put up with him for years and, anyway, he's in London most of the time. Oh well, one more of life's unsolved mysteries. And, I must say, if I have to have much to do with Annie Roberts, Diana won't be the only one turning to drink!"

CHAPTER SIX

I had the letters photocopied and rang Annie to arrange a time to see her. There was no reply so I gratefully put the matter to one side. But after a few days I thought I'd better go to call on her before she started to persecute me about them. As I drove cautiously along the narrow road to Mere Barton, I had to back awkwardly for quite a way to let an ambulance get by, so I was feeling a little flustered when I parked the car by the hotel and walked up the village street. When I approached, I saw that a few people had gathered outside Annie's house. They were in deep conversation, but as I came up to them Judith Lamb turned and greeted me.

"Isn't it terrible, Sheila — have you heard?"

"Heard what?" I said.

"Poor Annie — oh, it's so awful . . ."

"What's happened?" I asked. "Something

to do with Annie? Is she ill?"

"Very ill," Jim Fletcher said. "Some sort of stomach upset, but very serious. They've just taken her to hospital."

"How dreadful. Was it a bug of some kind?"

"We don't know yet. It's been going on for a couple of days now. Judith found her on Monday in a terrible state."

"She'd been so ill," Judith said. "You know, sickness and so forth. She was really weak and still had quite a lot of pain, but she wouldn't let me call the doctor, said it would go off, and told me not to stay. Well, you can imagine how I felt, leaving her like that, but she insisted."

"How awful," I said.

"Yes, it was. I didn't know what to do for the best. I rang Jim here and he said leave her for a bit and then he and Mary would call the next day and see how she was."

"We did call," he said, "but she didn't let us in — just called out to say that she was all right."

"But she *wasn't* all right," Judith broke in. "She was dreadfully bad in the night and when I called in this morning I said I didn't care what she said, I'd ring Dr. Macdonald, and, really, by then she wasn't in any fit state to stop me! Well, I was just on my way into my house to phone when I saw Lewis Chapman passing in the street. He took one look at her and called an ambulance — he's going with her to the hospital. They've only just gone."

"I passed an ambulance on my way here," I said. "That must have been them."

"It was so lucky Dr. Chapman was around," Jim Fletcher said. "If we'd had to wait for someone to come out from the surgery, we'd have been waiting still!"

"Oh, he was so good," Judith said. "Such a nice man, knew in a moment what to do."

"A real professional." Captain Prosser, who had been silent up to now, made his contribution. "That's what you need in a crisis. Someone who knows what he's doing. Amateurs can sometimes make things worse."

"Well, I don't think we did that," Judith said indignantly. "We did what would could — Annie wouldn't let us do any more."

"You can't force help on people," Jim said, "especially someone as strong-minded as Annie."

"Oh, I wasn't suggesting . . ." Captain Prosser said hastily, "not for a moment."

"What's the matter?" Rachel had joined the group. "Is something wrong?"

"It's Annie," Judith said, and began to tell

her story again.

"How awful," Rachel said. "It sounds really nasty. Thank goodness Lewis had the sense to get her to hospital."

"I did think of calling you to look at her," Judith said, "since you used to be a nurse and so on, but Annie was so set on no one coming."

"Actually I wasn't here then. Phyll and I have been down in Dorset, visiting Father's cousin." She turned to me. "You remember Grace, Grace Armitage — it was her ninetieth birthday so we felt we ought to be there. I'm so sorry about Annie, but I'm sure hospital is the best place for her just now."

"I wonder," Judith said, gesturing towards Annie's door, "if perhaps I'd better just go in to see if things are all right — no fires left on and so forth. And" — she lowered her voice — "see if there's any clearing up to do, if you know what I mean. I wouldn't like her to come back from hospital to anything like that."

"What a good idea," Rachel said. "Shall I come and give you a hand?"

"Oh, that would be marvelous," Judith said gratefully, "if you don't mind."

They went into the house and Jim Fletcher said, "Well, I suppose I'd better be getting along. Mary sent me up to the shop to get some bread — she'll be wondering where I've got to."

"I suppose I might as well go and get a few things from the shop as well," I said. "I really came to see Annie about the Book — some old letters. I don't know what will happen about it now."

"Well, of course you'll go on with it," Captain Prosser said briskly. "Annie will want to know how it's going when she gets back. I think I'll come with you. Maurice won't know what's happening."

Indeed, the exciting presence of an ambulance in the village had drawn a few people into the shop, the usual center of news and information. I remained silent while Jim and Captain Prosser (antiphonally) told their story, embellished with their feelings and reactions and prognostications as to the outcome.

"One of these superbugs, do you think?" Maurice asked. "There's a lot of them about."

"Or food poisoning," Jim suggested.

"That's not very likely," Margaret said, quick to defend the purity of the food on sale in the shop. "Nobody else in the village has gone down with anything like that."

"But," Jim persisted, "you know what Annie's like. She uses up every scrap of everything — stuff she's cooked days before. Mary went in there once and found her hotting up some meat left over from a joint that must have been a good week old! It's a miracle to me something like this hasn't happened before."

We all nodded wisely. Annie's frugality ("I can't abide waste. 'Waste not, want not.' That's what my mother used to say.") was a byword in the village as well as her contempt for those who ate ready meals or never used up leftovers.

"She cooks in batches," Jim went on. "She says it saves electricity — which it does, of course, but there are limits."

"And now," Margaret said, "since she was given that microwave, she just hots things up all the time. That's not healthy, surely!"

"There's nothing like good fresh home-cooked food," Captain Prosser (who considered himself something of an expert cook) said firmly.

We were all silent for a moment to consider the truth of this statement.

"Oh well," I said tritely, "she's in the best place now."

Enid Stevens, who, with her husband, Norman, runs the hotel and who's had some lively run-ins with Annie over the years, gave a little laugh. "Well, I wouldn't want to be one of the nurses looking after her," she said. "She'll drive them mad, telling them how much better things were done in her day!"

"She certainly won't be an easy patient," Margaret said. "That's for sure."

As I came out of the shop, I saw Rachel.

"How was everything?" I asked.

"Things were in a bit of a mess, so we've sorted that and locked up properly. Judith has the keys. Oh, and she packed up some nightgowns and toilet things — Phyll and I will take them into the hospital tomorrow and see how she is."

"Has Annie got any relatives?" I asked. "She never spoke about anyone."

"Not that I know of. I believe there were no other members of the family, apart from Annie, at the funeral when her mother died."

"How sad."

"I suppose so," Rachel said, "but I've never thought of Annie as sad exactly! She drives us all mad most of the time, but, really, she's the heart of the village."

"That's true," I said. "Anyway, how was Grace? I can't believe she's ninety."

"Oh, full of beans. Still very active. She bought a new car the other day."

"No!"

"Typical of Grace. It was a lovely party — a real mix of people from teenagers to other ninety-year-olds — lunch party, because she likes to play bridge in the evenings. I suspect that's why she was so keen for us to stay on for a few days, to make up numbers for her bridge."

"Good heavens, it makes me exhausted just to think of it."

"That generation is tough as old boots," Rachel said. "Think of Rosemary's mother!"

I was just washing out some cat food tins to go into the salvage, watched intently by Foss, who hoped it might inspire me to open another one, when the phone rang.

"I'm afraid Annie's in a pretty bad way," Rachel said. "She's in intensive care. Phyll and I weren't allowed to see her."

"Good heavens, what's the matter with her?"

"They wouldn't give us details because we're not relatives, but it does seem serious."

"How awful. Will she be all right?"

"Again, they wouldn't say, but I'd think it's touch and go. I'm going to try and phone Lewis; he might be able to find out more about her."

"Good idea. Do give me a ring when you

have any news."

All that morning I kept thinking about Annie and wondering how she was. As Rachel had said, she's the heart of the village and it's impossible to imagine Mere Barton without her.

"Oh, she'll recover," Rosemary said when we had lunch together. "She's a survivor, no question about that. Anyway, she's one of those small, wiry people, full of energy, who go on forever."

"I certainly hope so," I said. "From a purely selfish point of view I really need her help with this wretched book."

"How's it coming on?" Rosemary asked.

"Very slowly. In fact, I've barely started."

"I can't think why you agreed to do it in the first place."

"Because I'm an idiot," I said ruefully, "and because you know how difficult it is to say no to Annie — force of personality, I suppose. That's how she manages to get things done. And that's why I need her to bully people to produce material for the Book."

"What about those old letters of hers? Are they going to be useful?"

"I've had them photocopied but I haven't had a chance to read them yet. They're from her grandfather, written from France in the

First World War. I think he was a carpenter in the village, so they'll certainly go in."

"Has she anything else you could use?"

"I don't know, but I got the impression that there were other things, but, being Annie, she was going to disclose them one by one."

"You're going to need more than that," Rosemary said.

"I know; that's why I need Annie to badger people, not that there are many proper village people still around. Annie's going to write to some of them who've moved away — they might have stuff that would be useful. So you see why I need her back in the village!"

"I wonder what's wrong with her?" Rosemary said.

"The general impression is that it's some sort of food poisoning, but, of course, they wouldn't tell Rachel anything because she isn't a relative."

"That's maddening, especially as Annie doesn't seem to *have* any relatives."

It was quite late that evening when Rachel rang again. I'd fallen asleep in my chair in front of the television (something I'm increasingly prone to do) and was in that confused state that you are when jerked

90

suddenly into consciousness by the telephone.

"I'm afraid she's gone," Rachel said.

"Gone?" I echoed stupidly. "Gone where?"

"It's Annie. She died this afternoon. Lewis has just called me."

"Good heavens!" I was wide-awake now. "How awful."

"I think it was pretty inevitable, from what Lewis said."

"What was it?"

"An acute form of food poisoning. The effects lasted a few days and led to renal failure."

"Renal failure? That's kidneys, isn't it?"

"That was the problem. In the normal course of events it need not necessarily have proved fatal, but unfortunately it appears that Annie only had one kidney, so . . . well . . . that was that."

There was a moment's silence while I tried to take in what Rachel had been telling me.

"What sort of food poisoning?" I asked.

"We'll know more after the postmortem."

"A postmortem — oh dear!"

"Well," Rachel said patiently, "they have to establish the exact cause of death and there'll have to be an inquest, of course."

"Yes, I suppose so. It just sounds so horrible."

"It was a dreadful thing to have happened, but they do have to get to the bottom of it. Anyway, I thought you'd want to know as soon as possible, because of the Book and everything."

"Oh yes, of course — the Book. Well, thanks so much for letting me know . . ."

"I'd better get on; I need to tell other people in the village and I must see if I can get in touch with Father William. Perhaps we could have lunch sometime soon. Ask Rosemary."

There was the click on the phone and she was gone.

I thought of phoning Rosemary straightaway, but when I looked at the clock I saw it was quite late. So I took my confused and gloomy thoughts with me out into the kitchen and, while I was putting out the animals' supper and laying my tray, I wondered what effect Annie's death would have on the village and, indeed, what effect it would have on me.

"Oh dear, how dreadful," Rosemary said, "and what rotten luck about her only having one kidney. Did you know?"

"No, I don't think anyone did. You know

how Annie never talked about herself. I mean, she talked all the time about what she'd done and what she thought about everything — especially that! — but never any really personal details. Like why she'd never married, or, indeed, if she had any relatives — things like that."

"Now you come to mention it, she didn't, did she? We were all so occupied in seeing how involved she was in other people's lives that we never noticed things like that about her."

"I mean, we know she was the local midwife for years," I said, "but I haven't the faintest idea where she trained or where, if anywhere, she worked before she came back here."

"So need you go on with the Book now that Annie's not there to chivvy you?" Rosemary asked.

"That was one of the first things that occurred to me," I admitted. "Though I felt a bit guilty thinking it."

"I don't see why. You didn't want to do the thing in the first place and I don't expect there's anyone else in the village who cares about it either way."

"I don't expect there is."

But apparently we were wrong. Just after I'd spoken to Rosemary, Father William telephoned.

"Ah, Sheila, I gather Rachel has told you the sad news?" His voice, I noticed, was in clerical mode, soft and muted. "We are all very shocked and saddened by poor Annie's passing."

"Yes, it's dreadful, isn't it. Is there any news about when the funeral is to be?"

"No, alas, we have to wait for the postmortem and then, perhaps, for the inquest — it depends on what the findings will be — before any decision can be made."

"Oh dear."

"I have made myself responsible for the arrangements, since there do not seem to be any relations. And because of that, there will, of course, be a lot to do." The tone was now brisker with just a slight undertone of importance. "But I have been thinking about what *kind* of service she would have wished for, so I am asking all her friends to get in touch with me if they have any suggestions."

"Well," I said hesitantly, "I have no idea what Annie thought about such things. I really didn't know her that well."

"But you have been working with her on that splendid book, which will, in some ways, be her memorial!"

"Oh, I wouldn't say that."

"Something she cared about so much!"

"I don't know if I *can* go on with it. There were a lot of things Annie was going to do."

"I'm sure you'll find a way — you're so resourceful — and it's the last tribute the village can pay to her."

There was much more in a similar vein, and when he'd finally rung off I slammed around the kitchen in a temper.

"It's absolutely ridiculous and I don't see why I should be lumbered with it!" I said to Tris, who looked at me with his head on one side, worried by my cross voice. "All that tiresome work — and I don't even *live* in the wretched village!" I said to Foss, sitting impassively on top of the microwave. "Even when she's dead, Annie Roberts is forcing me to do things I don't want to do. It isn't fair!"

Foss gave me a contemptuous stare, jumped down and stalked off into the hall where I could hear him sharpening his claws on the stair carpet.

CHAPTER SEVEN

I got out the photocopies I'd made of Annie's letters, because I still didn't like to work from the originals, and began to look through them. I've read quite a few letters written home by soldiers (including those from my father when he was a chaplain in Italy during the last war) and I'm always struck by the fact that, almost always, even in the most horrible places and at times of great stress and danger, the language is so matter of fact. I suppose it's an instinctive shying away from heroics.

Frank Roberts's letters were like that. Written from a position just outside Ypres, the commonplace words (designed to keep from his family any knowledge of the appalling conditions around him) were very touching. Now that we've all seen on television pictures of the unspeakable horror of mud and devastation, the words "a bit wet and miserable" and "not exactly a home from home" were immensely moving. As were the references to the children, about how much they'd have grown, so that he wouldn't recognize them when he got back.

Fortunately Frank Roberts did go back and took up his old job as village carpenter, just as if he'd never been away. And I believe he never referred to those years, except to make the odd joke with a fellow ex-soldier, down at the Legion, about lorries that should have brought ammunition being full of plum and apple jam, and to say, on occasion, that he didn't think much of foreign parts. I would have liked to ask Annie what memories she had of her grandfather — he seems to have been a mild and kindly man who would have been fond of his grandchild — but now it was too late. I would just have to imagine it. Though it was hard, almost impossible, to imagine Annie as a child.

On an impulse, I put the letters away, got out the car and went to Mere Barton. Having no plan in mind I went into the shop, the most likely place to glean what information there was about Annie. Maurice was behind the counter, deep in conversation with Judith. He looked up as I came in.

"Sheila might be able to help," he said. "Her son is — was — Annie's solicitor." He turned to me. "That's right, isn't it?"

"Yes, he is," I said, "but I don't know . . ."

"It's so awkward," Judith said. "I really don't know what to do — it's the keys, you see. Now that poor Annie's gone, who should I give them to? I mean, I'm quite happy to hang on to them for the time being, but I wouldn't want to do the wrong thing — legally, that is. What *is* the situation? I don't know of any relatives, do you? And what's to become of all her things? She had some very nice pieces — that dresser in the kitchen (it's a really old Welsh dresser, you know, and they're fetching a good price at auction. I saw one on television the other day) and that bookcase in the sitting room — lots of things. What's to become of those?"

"I'm afraid I don't know," I said. "I haven't spoken to Michael since Annie died — he and the family are away for a few days — but I'm sure if you rang the practice, they'd advise you —"

"It's the responsibility," Judith went on. "As I said, I'd be happy to hang on to the keys, but I would like to know . . . well, what's going to happen."

"Do we know what the result of the postmortem is," I asked, "and if there's got to be an inquest? If there is, I suppose the police would have to be involved."

"No, we haven't heard," Maurice said. "We're waiting for Lewis — I don't suppose they'd tell us, would they?"

"I'd be happy to give them to the police," Judith said, "if that's what they want. I had been going to go in there to water the plants, but now — well, I don't think . . . I mean, she had some really nice potted plants, and it would be a shame just to let them die. But I don't like to actually go *in,* not with Annie — you know . . ."

"It is awkward," I said. "I have those letters of hers — her grandfather's, that is. She gave them to me for the Book, but now . . ."

"Oh, you'll go on with the Book," Judith exclaimed. "It's what she would have wanted. Don't you think so, Maurice? Oh, you must go on!"

"It's really a question of who the letters belong to now," I said, "and, if I do go on with it, Annie said there are other things she had that ought to go in as well. I really don't know what to do about them."

"It seems to me," Maurice said, "that there's not much that we can do until we know what's in the will — I suppose she did make a will?" He looked at me inquiringly.

"I don't know," I said. "I suppose she must have done, though often people don't."

"There's the cottage," Maurice said thoughtfully. "That was Annie's. I mean, it belonged to her mother and she left it to her. Her father was in the army, killed in the war, in North Africa I think it was, though Annie never talked about it. So there was a widow's pension and her mother used to work at the hotel and, then, Annie was earning. I never knew the mother, of course; she died before we came here. Anyhow, as I was saying, there's the cottage. That must be worth quite a bit — properties in the village are fetching ridiculous amounts. I was just saying to Margaret the other day, it's lucky we bought this place when we did; we certainly couldn't have afforded it now!"

"Of course," Judith said, "Mere Barton is a very desirable village — do you know I heard that Pitlands Farm sold for the best part of a million — and there isn't any land now, just the house!"

"So who gets Annie's cottage, then?" Maurice said. "If there are no relatives — and what if she didn't make a will? Does the government get it?"

"Oh, that wouldn't be fair," Judith said indignantly, "coming and taking people's *property* like that. They couldn't, could they?"

They both looked at me as if being the mother of a solicitor gave me some sort of legal competence.

I shook my head. "I really don't know . . . ," I began, when the door opened and Lewis came in.

We all turned to him eagerly and Maurice said, "Now, here's somebody who can tell us what's what."

"Have they had the result of the postmortem?" I asked.

He nodded. "Yes. It's as we thought — food poisoning."

"Do they know what caused it?" Maurice asked quickly, anxious, no doubt, for the reputation of the shop.

"It seems to have been some sort of fungus," Lewis said.

"Oh well!" Maurice said, visibly relieved. "We might have known it! All those toadstools and stuff she used to gather in the woods —"

"I was *always* nervous about her eating them," Judith broke in. "Time and again I said to her, 'Annie, are you sure they're safe?' but she never listened to me. Once, she gave me some in a bag, told me to fry them just like proper mushrooms. Well, I thanked her, of course, but when I got home I threw them away, and when she asked me I said they were delicious!"

"It's strange, though," I said. "Annie was very knowledgeable about such things; how did she come to make such a terrible mistake?"

"Oh, that kitchen of hers," Judith said, "very dark, with that tiny window, and she never had the light on in the daytime. Too careful of the electricity, I suppose."

"Well," Maurice said, "if she'd been more careful over what she was cooking, this would never have happened!"

"But still . . . ," I said.

"And her eyesight wasn't too good," Judith said. "Half the time she never wore her glasses — and now you see what that led to."

I turned to Lewis. "I suppose there'll have to be an inquest?"

"Yes. I saw Inspector Morris at the hospital. He'll be coming to look round the house. I told him that the cottage was safely locked up and that you, Judith, had the keys, so he'll be calling on you soon."

"I'm sure I'll be glad to hand them over," Judith said. "Such a responsibility. I wonder: Do you think he'd mind if I just went in with him and watered the plants?"

■ ■ ■ ■

The inquest was held quite quickly and the verdict (to no one's surprise) was accidental death. Apparently fungi had been found in the basket in the kitchen, and some of them were discovered to be poisonous. An expert, called in to give evidence, said it was possible that the *Lepiota* specimens found in the house might have been confused with the *Macrolepiota* form, which is edible. Expressions of regret were made all round, and warnings of the danger of having insufficient knowledge of the subject would have annoyed Annie very much.

What did surprise everyone was the will. Annie had left everything to a cousin we'd none of us ever heard of, who lived in London.

"Some man," Michael said when he called to deliver some eggs, "called Martin Stillwell — living in Acton."

"What's he like?" I asked.

"He seems like an ordinary sort of person," Michael said.

"What sort of ordinary?"

"Just . . . ordinary. Well," he elaborated, seeing my look, "late fifties, medium height, um . . . oh yes, a widower, no children, works for a travel company. He called in at the office and I brought him up to speed on what had happened. Actually, he said he didn't know Annie at all and only met her once when they were children and her mother took her up to London for a couple of days and they stayed with his family."

"Goodness, how extraordinary. I suppose she left him everything — I guess it was everything? — because he was the only relative."

"Yes, I suppose so. And yes, she did leave him everything, except the Welsh dresser in the kitchen; she left that to Judith."

"Fancy! Judith will be pleased. So how long's he staying down here?"

"Only a couple of days. He wants to be here for the funeral, of course, but he's got to go abroad for his firm — Greece, I think he said — almost immediately."

"Oh. Do you think I could see him? Is he staying at the cottage?"

"No, he said he'd rather not. He's been to see it, of course, but he's actually staying at the Westfield here in Taviscombe."

"Well, he can't be too badly off," I said. "The Westfield's quite expensive. It's just that I wanted to ask him about those letters Annie lent me and see if he'd mind looking for the other stuff she was going to let me have for the Book."

"Why don't you go and see him at the Westfield; he said he'd be in this afternoon."

Michael was right; Martin Stillwell was ordinary. That is, he looked like any middle-aged, middle-class businessman in a neat gray suit, with what looked like a club tie. I could see no sort of resemblance to Annie. He had a quiet but pleasant manner, and I explained the situation and asked him about the letters.

"Oh, I'd very much like to see them sometime. Let me see — Frank Roberts? My grandmother was a Roberts; she must have been his sister. That's right; there were two boys, Frank and Bert — they joined up together, but Bert was killed near Amiens — and three girls, Amy, Jane and Lily. Lily was my grandmother on my father's side. That makes Annie my second cousin." He looked at me and smiled. "As you'll have gathered, I'm interested in family history. I knew my grandmother came from the West Country and I always meant to visit and find out some more. I'm really sorry I never knew Annie properly; she could have filled me in on all sorts of things."

"Annie wasn't much of a one for talking about her family," I said cautiously, startled by this sudden animation.

"Really? What was she like?"

I thought for a moment, wondering how to describe Annie without dwelling on her all too obvious faults. "Someone once said she was the heart of the village," I said. "She ran most of the village affairs — of course, she knew everyone. She used to be the local district nurse, though they call them something different now. She was a great organizer. This book about the village, for instance, that was her idea."

"It sounds like a splendid idea, just the sort of thing that every village should be doing. We ought to be gathering memories of the past before they're gone forever. I'll really look forward to seeing it. And, of course, anything I can do to help — well, I'd be delighted."

"Thank you so much," I said gratefully. "Perhaps we could meet at the cottage before you go back and I could give you the originals of the letters and, if you wouldn't mind looking among her papers and so on for the things she thought might be useful . . ."

"As I said, I'd be delighted. Tomorrow, then, about eleven, if that's all right with you."

When I arrived at the cottage he was already there. Although he'd put on an electric fire the place felt damp and miserable and had a bleak, empty feeling that made me very aware of the fact that Annie was no longer there. He had some papers spread out on the table.

"She didn't seem to have a desk, but I found these in the drawers of the sideboard. I haven't looked through them yet, but I don't think there's anything there that you might want. They're mostly receipted bills and papers about some sort of trust she was involved in."

"Oh yes, I know about that. My son, Michael — I think you met him — is another of the trustees."

"I haven't looked upstairs," he said. "Shall we go up and see if there's anything there?"

It felt strange going into Annie's bedroom. I hung back at the door, feeling I had no right to be invading her privacy, but Martin Stillwell was standing behind me, so I had to go in.

It was a typical cottage room, with a sloping ceiling that minimized what space there was, almost filled by a large old-fashioned double bed covered with a heavy white bedspread. There was a small table beside the bed with a lamp and a book standing on an embroidered cloth. I was curious to see what the book was, but didn't like to examine it while someone else was there.

A built-in cupboard and a small chest at the foot of the bed completed the furnishings. There was no dressing table and no mirror. It was an austere room, its plainness relieved only by the unexpected pale blue carpet and curtains, but they were faded and may well have been her mother's taste. Martin Stillwell opened the cupboard that held clothes — garments I'd seen her wear over the years.

"Nothing there," he said. "Perhaps the chest?"

We both edged round the end of the bed and he opened the chest. It was full of papers, some in files, some in broken-sided cardboard boxes, some loose.

"Good heavens," he said. "It's going to take a very long time to go through that lot!"

"I'm afraid you're right," I agreed.

"There's no way I can go through all that while I'm down here now. But you knew Annie, you're an old friend, and I imagine you'd really like to get on with this book. So, how would it be if I gave you a spare key — I've got one here — so you can come in and see for yourself if there's anything that might be useful to you?"

"Well," I said cautiously, "I've certainly known Annie for some years, though I'd hardly call myself a friend, and I suppose it would be the simplest thing to do, if you're sure that's all right with you. I'll return the key to you as soon as I've looked through the papers."

He smiled. "That's fine by me." He closed the lid of the chest. "Is there anywhere round here where we could get a cup of coffee? I don't exactly fancy using anything there might be in the kitchen!"

"There's the hotel," I said, "down the road."

Enid was surprised to see us. "Annie's cousin, is it? I heard you were down here. Are you staying long? Such a tragedy it was — we all miss her, everyone in the village . . ."

She bustled about getting the coffee, chatting as she went. When we were finally alone he said, "I was wondering, Mrs. Malory, if you'd very kindly help me with something?"

"Yes, of course, if I can. And do say Sheila, please."

"Thank you, and I'm Martin. Well, the

fact is, I have to make arrangements for the funeral and I haven't the faintest idea of what would be suitable; there was nothing about it in the will. The clergyman here, Father something, I didn't catch his name, seemed to take it for granted that there would be a service in the church and a burial in the churchyard. Would that be what she would have wished?"

"Oh yes, I'm sure she would."

"And what about hymns and so forth —" He broke off and I saw that he was staring at someone who'd just come in. It was Phyll.

CHAPTER EIGHT

Phyll came towards us. "Hello, Sheila," she said. "Enid told me you were in the lounge." She turned to look at Martin, who had got to his feet when she approached. For a moment she didn't say anything; then she put out her hand. "Martin," she said, "how nice to see you."

"Do join us," I said. "I gather you two know each other."

"Yes," Phyll said. "We met some years ago — fancy your being Annie's cousin."

I looked inquiringly at Martin and he said, "It was in Madeira; Phyllis was there with her father and I was with a tour — I was standing in for one of our reps."

"I'll just go and ask Enid to bring some more coffee," I said, and left the room reluctantly, curious to know what they would have to say to each other after such a long time. Enid maddeningly detained me with chatter about coincidences, so that when I got back and Enid had brought some more coffee, their first greetings were over.

"Dr. Craig helped me out of a very difficult situation," Martin said. "I'd taken a party to see some rather special gardens, and one of the group, an elderly gentleman, was taken ill — it turned out to be a heart attack, though *I* had no idea at the time. But, being a doctor, he very kindly took over and identified the problem and went with us to the hospital while Phyllis" — he turned to her and smiled — "very kindly took over in her turn and organized the rest of the day and got them all back to the hotel. A brilliant exercise in logistics!"

"Oh, that was nothing compared to taking the lower fifth on a school trip!" Phyll said. "Are you still with the same company?" she asked.

"Yes, I am, but now I check out new resorts and hotels and they send me out as a sort of troubleshooter if there's a problem."

"I should think you'd be good at that."

They seemed to be very much at ease with each other, though that didn't surprise me because Phyll usually got on well with people, and I suppose he had to in his particular job.

"I was just asking Mrs. Malory — Sheila — for help with the funeral service," Martin said. "What do you suggest?"

"Oh, I think Annie would want something conventional," Phyll said. "Don't you think so, Sheila?"

"I'm sure she would."

"And certainly the proper prayer book service — that's what Father William always uses, and the King James Bible. I know how annoyed she was whenever he was away and the locum used that modern version and the New English Bible!"

"Well, that's settled, then," Martin said, "except for the hymns and the psalm."

"Oh, the twenty-third psalm," I said. "Though if we have that, then I suppose we can't have the George Herbert hymn."

"We could have 'Abide with Me,' " Phyll suggested. "Or do they sing it at football matches now?"

"They used to have 'Rock of Ages' when I was a boy," Martin said. "Would that be too old-fashioned?"

"What about 'Dear Lord and Father of Mankind'?" Phyll said. "Most people know that. I mean, you've got to have hymns people know, else the singing sounds so thin."

"There's the other George Herbert

hymn," I said. " 'Teach Me My God and King' — it's one of my favorites, and I'm sure Annie would like the bit about sweeping a room. Or we could have 'Praise My Soul, the King of Heaven'; that's pretty safe." It suddenly occurred to me that we were turning it into a sort of parlor game. "Anyway," I said, turning to Martin, "I'm sure Father William will have some suggestions. When are you going to see him?"

"This afternoon. I really need to get the arrangements made as soon as possible because I have to get back to London pretty soon."

"If you're going to see him this afternoon," Phyll said, "why don't you come and have lunch with us? I'm sure Rachel would love to meet you."

"That would be very nice, thank you."

I looked at my watch. "Goodness, is that the time? I must be moving." As I got up, Martin pulled a key ring from his pocket and detached a key.

"Here's the spare key," he said. "Keep it as long as you want."

"Oh, I won't need it for long," I said. "I can give it back to you after the funeral. And you'll be coming down again, I expect, so that I can return the papers to you when I've finished with them."

"Oh yes," he said. "I'll hope to be coming down as soon as I get back from Greece."

As I got back to my car I thought with some amusement of how Phyll hadn't included me in the lunch invitation, though I was pretty sure she would have done if I'd been on my own.

I wondered whether there had been some sort of holiday romance between them — though that didn't seem like Phyll, especially if she'd been there with her father. No, obviously they had just got on well together and it was nice that they had met again so fortuitously, and if something more developed, that would be nice too.

More or less all the village turned out for Annie's funeral. People don't send flowers nowadays, so there was only one wreath (presumably Martin's) of white lilies on the coffin and a plate at the back of the church for donations to the local hospice. The altar flowers were particularly fine — more lilies and great heavy-headed chrysanthemums. "Judith did the flowers," Phyll had said as we came in. Father William spoke the service beautifully, his mellifluous voice seeming to soar up to the barrel roof with its carved finials, so that I found myself listening to the sound, as if to a piece of music, rather than to what he was actually saying. I did catch snatches of his eulogy: ". . . an irreplaceable loss to the village . . . ," ". . . her untiring work . . . ," and ". . . an unusual and refreshing personality." Rosemary nudged me at this. And then it was all over and we were in the village hall and there were refreshments, so that I was reminded of how, such a short time ago, we'd been gathered together here on another occasion.

"Marvelous food," Rosemary said to Rachel, who with Phyll and Captain Prosser had joined us. "Who did it?"

"Oh, we all rallied round," Rachel said.

"It was a splendid turnout," I said.

"Well, we had to give the old girl a good send-off," the captain said, and I thought what a withering put-down Annie would have given him at such familiarity. "Excellent service — no Series Three nonsense. You can rely on Father William to do a proper job."

"There wasn't a plot in the churchyard next to her mother," Phyll said, "so they had to put her in the new bit, at the back, but, as Martin said, it's a peaceful spot, and there you get the view all down the valley."

I wondered who would enjoy the view, since Annie could not. Perhaps Martin would come and visit her grave occasionally. He joined us then and I introduced him to Rosemary.

"Thank you so much for coming," he said to us. "I never knew her, of course, but I'm sure she would have appreciated it."

"She'd certainly have expected us all to be on parade," Captain Prosser said. "A stickler for the right thing, Annie was."

"So I gather." Martin permitted himself a slight smile as if in tribute to his unknown cousin, and we were all silent for a moment.

Meanwhile a buzz of conversation had built up as people began to move towards the refreshments, fill their plates with food and form little animated groups about the hall.

"Well, I don't know about you," Captain Prosser said, "but I'm going to get some of those sausage rolls before they've all gone. Actually," he said confidentially to me as we made our way towards the tables, "if I make a good meal here, I shan't bother to cook tonight."

Father William was by the refreshment table holding a cup of tea. He lifted his hand in salutation when he saw me.

"The cup that cheers but not inebriates," he said. "But I suppose four o'clock in the afternoon is a little early for anything stronger, even if some people may feel the need for it."

"A lovely service," I said. "I'm sure it was just what Annie would have liked."

"Certainly," he said, "she liked a good funeral. I can't remember her missing one in all the years I've been here. Presumably she wished to keep tabs on people in death as well as in life."

I gave an involuntary smile and said, "I suppose she did always like to know what was going on, but I don't think you could say that she was a gossip."

"No, Annie just liked the knowledge; she had no wish to spread it around."

"She'll be greatly missed," I said conventionally.

"You think so? Personally I feel that most people in the village will be rather relieved not to have her looking over their collective shoulder."

"But what about all the things she did, all the things she organized!"

"Don't you feel that other people might have wished to organize things too?"

"But she was so good at getting people to do things."

"She certainly had a way about her."

I felt uncomfortably as though I was engaged in some sort of verbal rally with him and was glad when Toby Parker came up behind us.

"Splendid effort, Father," he greeted him. "Felt I must get down here to pay my last respects. Diana sent her apologies, by the way — nasty migraine. Nice to see the church so full."

"Hello, Toby," I said. "Sorry to hear about Diana."

He looked a little uneasy, perhaps remembering the last time we had been together.

"So," he continued, "what's all this about a long-lost cousin who's suddenly appeared out of the blue?"

"His name is Martin Stillwell," I said, "and that's him over there, talking to Judith."

"Most extraordinary. And she never mentioned him to anyone?"

"No. We only heard about him because of the will."

"Pretty mysterious, if you ask me."

"God moves in a mysterious way," Father William said. "Perhaps that was a hymn we should have had." He smiled and moved away.

Toby looked after him. "He gets more peculiar every time I see him," he said. "But, anyway, do I gather that this chap gets the lot?"

"Well, except for the Welsh dresser, yes, he does."

"Welsh dresser? Oh, never mind — he gets the cottage?"

"Yes."

"And what about the contents?"

"He gets those as well — except, as I said, the Welsh dresser. She left that to Judith."

He looked as if he was about to say something but, with a muttered excuse, he turned away in the direction of Martin Stillwell. I was amused to see how skillfully he extricated him from Judith's stream of conversation and edged him into a corner of the hall where they were unlikely to be disturbed. Judith, balked of one listener and catching my eye, came over.

"What a lovely lot of people. The church was nearly full, and Maurice told me that the donations came to over £50 — such a good cause; I'm sure Annie would be pleased."

"Very gratifying."

"And Mr. Stillwell, such a nice man, so friendly. He told me how grateful he was for all I did when poor Annie was so ill, and afterwards, looking after things. Well, I said, it was the least I could do, after all these years. And he was very nice about the Welsh dresser — he said he was so pleased that she'd remembered me, which was good of him, really, because it would have probably have made quite a sum at auction. They're very collectible, you know — not that I'd ever sell it, of course."

"Of course not," I agreed.

"Anyway, he said I was to let him know when I wanted it moved into *my* cottage and he'd arrange for a man to come and do it. Wasn't that kind! But, actually, I do need to have my own kitchen redecorated soon. There's dampness coming in by the back door, so I've decided to have a complete rearrangement — a makeover, that's what they call it now, isn't it? That means I must think how to fit the dresser in. I mean, it's quite big, so I'll have to move the cupboard next to the sink — actually I suppose I might get rid of it." She leaned confidentially towards me. "It's got woodworm, you know, and I wouldn't like that to spread to the dresser. So I told Mr. Stillwell that I'll leave it for a bit until all that's been sorted."

"It all sounds most exciting," I said, backing away, "but do excuse me; I need to have a quick word with Mr. Stillwell before I go."

Toby had disappeared and Martin was now being buttonholed by Captain Prosser in Ancient Mariner mode.

". . . and then I was stationed in Malta —

amazing place. Have you ever been there?"

"Yes, I know it quite well."

"Oh really —"

"Do excuse me for interrupting," I said, "but if I could just have a word with you, Martin."

"Of course," he said gratefully as we moved away. "How can I help you?"

"It's just to say that I haven't been able to get the papers from Annie's cottage yet, so would you mind if I held on to the key for a little while longer?"

"Of course not; there's no rush," he said. "I'm in no hurry to do anything about the cottage, so please do take your time."

"Oh, thank you. That would be marvelous." I paused and then I asked, "Are you going to sell the cottage? You don't fancy living there yourself?"

"The thought had crossed my mind. I'd keep my London flat, of course — I need to be in London at present for my work — but I'll be retiring soon and this is an attractive village and the people seem very friendly."

"That would be splendid," I said. "Even though you never knew Annie, it would be nice to think of the cottage staying in the family!"

"Well, he seems very nice," Rosemary said

as we drove home, "and I see what you mean about him and Phyll — almost as if they're old friends. Anyway, it was a good turnout for the funeral and afterwards. Fancy Toby coming down!"

"I know. In the end it was quite a jolly affair."

"Did it strike you, though," Rosemary asked, "that there was a sort of sense of relief?"

"You're right; there was. Actually that's exactly what Father William said — as if everyone was relieved not to have her looking over their shoulder all the time."

"Oh dear, what a way to be remembered!"

"You must admit she did rather loom over the village — the way she ran everything."

"I wonder who'll do that now?" Rosemary asked. "Perhaps Rachel will."

"Well, it might be a good occupation for her, and *she* would do it in the nicest possible way!"

CHAPTER NINE

A few days later, spurred on by my conversation with Martin Stillwell, I decided to go and collect the papers from Annie's cottage. I thought I'd better go into the shop first and announce my intentions, since there would be endless speculation if anyone saw me (as someone certainly would) going into the cottage.

Fortunately, Judith was at the counter, talking to Maurice, and I knew that she would spread the reason for my visit better than anyone.

"I'll just have some stamps," Judith was saying. "A book of first class, please, before they go up again, and can you tell me how much it will be to send this letter to Ireland — that's Dublin, not the northern bit. My old friend Sally Davis — she married an Irishman. There were such problems because he was a Catholic and she wasn't, but his family came round in the end, and he died last year and I thought she might have come back to England, but she said no, she couldn't stand the upheaval . . ."

Maurice took the letter and withdrew to the other side of the shop where the post office was and I said to Judith, "I'm just going into Annie's cottage — Martin gave me a spare key — to get the papers we found, the ones Annie promised me for the Book."

"Would you like me to come with you?" she asked eagerly.

"Not really," I said hastily. "I might be a little while because I need to sort out which ones will be suitable."

"Yes, of course. It's just that I thought you might not like to be in there by yourself after — well, you know . . ."

"That's very kind of you," I said, "but I'll be fine."

Since Maurice was coming back, I was able to make my escape and walked up the street to the cottage. When I went in, the dank, oppressive feeling was even greater than when I was there with Martin, so that, just for a minute, I wished I'd accepted Judith's offer. But I pulled myself together and went upstairs.

As I had before, I paused on the threshold of the bedroom; it seemed even more of an intrusion now that I was by myself. But then, looking into the room, I saw the book on the table beside the bed and curiosity propelled me forwards. When I picked it up I was astonished to see that it was the recently published memoirs of a prominent businessman. As I retrieved a till receipt that fell out, I saw it was from our local branch of Smith's. I wondered what could have prompted Annie to have paid £20 for such a book. I looked with bewilderment at the photograph of the author on the front of the shiny new book jacket, a stern, purposeful face, but with secret, watchful eyes. But then, I knew nothing of Annie's reading habits; perhaps this was the sort of thing she habitually read.

I looked round the room in search of other books. There was none in this room, but in the other, smaller bedroom, furnished with a single bed, wardrobe and a chest of drawers, I found a few on the broad window ledge, between two pottery bookends. There were a couple of old books on Exmoor, a hunting book by Cecil Aldin, *The English Hymnal,* and a copy of Tennyson's *Poems,* bound in limp leather, worn and crumbling at the edges. I picked it up and opened it. There was a handsome bookplate inside inscribed *Martha Cross. For Good Attendance. Easter 1895.* It was signed *Harriet*

Percy. I looked at it with interest; presumably it had belonged to Annie's mother and had been given to her by the very Miss Percy whose trust Annie was involved in. The symmetry of the situation was somehow pleasing. I replaced the book and went back into Annie's room.

The chest was, indeed, very full of papers. I cautiously lifted out one of the files. It contained old sepia photographs with faded writing on the back; some were in the form of postcards, something I remembered from similar ones in my own family. Another file had a miscellaneous collection of old newspaper cuttings, fragile and yellow with age. Yet another had actual postcards, views of seaside resorts with figures in old-fashioned clothes, buildings of various kinds, or sentimental ones with flowers or kittens, some decorated with glitter that fell away from my hand as I picked them up. It was obvious that I couldn't possibly sort them all out in situ — I'd have to take them home and deal with them there. I eased them carefully into the couple of shopping bags I'd brought with me, painfully straightened my back and stood up again.

Downstairs I went into the kitchen. It was tidy now (Judith and Rachel had done a good job of clearing up) and looked much as it had when I'd been there before. There was no sign of the basket that had contained the fungi. I assumed the police had taken it away. I went over to the back door and, on an impulse, clicked back the lock and went outside. The garden was quite small, but Annie always kept it looking very trim. Now, though, it was beginning to look overgrown and neglected. The tiny lawn needed cutting, and in the flower beds the late dahlias and asters were being smothered by grass and weeds. The small bed by the back door was closely planted with herbs, so that looked all right. I bent down and picked a piece of rosemary, crushing it in my hand and thinking ("Rosemary, that's for remembrance") of Annie.

I was startled by a sudden noise. The garden backed onto a field, and a horse, attracted by the sight of someone, had come up to the little gate in the fence. I went towards it, but it shied away and went cantering back to its companion grazing on the far side of the field.

I went back into the kitchen, carefully locking the door behind me. The Welsh dresser, now that I came to look at it, was, indeed, quite large, and I could quite see that Judith would have to make a fairly radical rearrangement to accommodate it. On an impulse I opened one of the drawers. It contained tablecloths, tea towels and other kitchen items, and I supposed Judith would inherit the contents as well as the dresser itself. When I tried to push the drawer back it stuck and, although I moved it from side to side, it wouldn't move. I put my hand inside and pulled out a piece of paper that had got wedged at the back and the drawer went back quite smoothly. The paper was crumpled and torn from my efforts to pull it out and I looked round for a bin or something to put it in, but I couldn't see one, so I stuffed it into my pocket and went along the passage back into the sitting room.

My eye was drawn to a small bookcase by the fireplace and I went over to look at it. I always think bookcases look rather sad when there are only a few books in them and the spaces have been filled with ornaments and photographs. There were a few gardening books, an early copy of Mrs. Beeton (probably quite valuable now), the illustrated history of a neighboring village (presumably where Annie got the idea for the Mere Barton book), a couple of paperbacks (ancient Penguins of *The Owl's House* and *The Lonely Plough*) and a large family Bible, which I opened and noted that the names of the family had been carefully inscribed with the dates of their births and deaths. I thought that Martin would be pleased to have that. But none of the books explained the book of memoirs beside Annie's bed. I picked up my shopping bags and, with a last look round the room, let myself out and locked the front door behind me.

As I stepped down into the street Judith's door opened — she'd obviously been waiting for me.

"Was everything all right?" she asked.

"Fine, thank you."

"And you found everything you wanted?"

"I think I've got all the papers Annie promised me," I said, holding up the shopping bags.

"Good gracious, I expect all that will keep you busy!"

"I expect it will."

"And everything was all right in the house?"

"It felt a bit cold and damp, but otherwise everything seemed fine."

She came down the steps from her front door and said confidentially, "*I've* got Annie's potted plants. Well, I did mention to Mr. Stillwell how worried I was about keeping them watered, and she had some very nice ones — that beautiful Christmas cactus, for instance, though that one doesn't need watering so often. She's had it for ages and it's grown enormous, so it really ought to be repotted. Anyway, I was telling Mr. Stillwell about all this and he asked me if I'd like to have them. Wasn't that kind!"

"I'm sure he'll be glad to know that you'll look after them."

"Potted plants are so *personal,* don't you think, more than plants in the garden. And, actually, I'm really worried about Annie's garden — it's getting quite overgrown. I just looked over the fence the other day and I was shocked to see how bad it was. I'm sure it would have grieved poor Annie to see it looking like that."

"I expect," I said soothingly, "Mr. Stillwell will be making some arrangement about it when he comes down."

"Oh, do you think so? Yes, I'm sure you're right — such a nice man. Now, while you're here, would you like to come in and have a cup of tea — or coffee?"

"That's very kind of you, but I really ought to be getting on with all this." I held up the shopping bags again. "Some other time, perhaps, I'd love to."

When I got home I certainly intended to start work on the papers, but by the time

I'd let the animals out and then fed them it was lunchtime. After lunch I had to go in to Brunswick Lodge because I'd rashly promised Anthea that I'd set out the chairs and help with the refreshments for a talk on discontinued local railways that she'd persuaded someone to give. By the time I got home all I had the energy for was to get supper and spend the evening slumped in front of the televison.

The following day was gray and rainy, miserable outside and appealingly warm and cozy inside, the sort of day, in fact, most conducive to work. I spread out some of the photographs on the dining room table. As I worked my way through them I became absorbed in my task — many of them would be invaluable. The changing face of the village street, with ancient cars and bicycles; a group of children at the village school, one of estate tenants and another of bell ringers, all taken in the 1890s; photographs of the football club and the cricket team sometime in the 1930s — many others of a similar nature. Finally, I found a photograph of a little girl (about eight years old) standing, shyly, just behind her mother, on the steps of a cottage. They both wore summer dresses, and both were staring self-consciously at the camera. It was only when

I read the writing on the back (*Martha and Annie, Whitsun 1954*) that I realized that the bashful child in the cotton frock, with a bow of ribbon in her straight fair hair, had grown up to be the Annie who had been such a forceful personality in the village. I sat for quite a while looking at it — a moment in time, one summer day in the early 1950s. The dining room clock striking twelve recalled me to the present and I hastily put the photographs back in their folder and went to get ready to have lunch with Rosemary.

"Well, at least I've made a start," I said, swishing the ice about in my spritzer. We usually go out when we have lunch together; it saves us both cooking. "There's masses of stuff — a whole chestful from Annie's."

"What was it like going in there?" Rosemary asked curiously.

"A bit daunting," I said. "Houses that haven't been lived in for a bit are always depressing, especially at this time of the year when it's been so wet and everything feels damp."

"Don't I know," Rosemary said forcibly. "Clothes in one of the wardrobes practically have mold growing on them — they'll all have to go to the dry cleaners. I suppose it's worse living in a house built of sandstone; it simply *absorbs* the moisture!"

"And, anyway," I continued, "you know what a strong personality Annie had. I felt like an intruder and half expected her to pop up at any minute and turn me out!"

"I think you were very brave; I wouldn't be surprised if she haunted the place."

"There was certainly a presence. Still, I got the papers and things. They were in a chest in her bedroom."

"What was it like — the bedroom, I mean?"

"Impersonal, a bit austere. I rather suspect she moved in there — the other bedroom's very small — after her mother died and didn't change a thing. Though . . ." I hesitated. "Though there was something that surprised me." And I told Rosemary about the book. "It really was most unexpected."

"How weird! Max Holtby, he's a top man in some oil business, isn't he?"

"That's right."

"Perhaps she'd been playing the stock market — no, that doesn't sound right. I wonder if there's something in his childhood . . . Perhaps she's his long-lost sister. After all, we don't know much about her family. Look how surprised we were when

134

Martin Stillwell popped up!"

"I must try and get hold of a copy of the book and see if there is anything."

"You should have borrowed Annie's."

"Oh, I couldn't do that! No, I'll see if I can get it from the library."

"I'll ask Mother," Rosemary said, "and see if she knows anything about the Roberts family. She'll know something, even if it's only gossip. Shall we order; can you see the menu on the blackboard from here? The fish pie was very good last time."

It started raining again when I got home, and I put my raincoat on to take the dustbin out and when I got back into the house I felt in my pocket for a tissue to wipe the rain off my glasses. Instead of a tissue I pulled out a piece of paper; it was the paper that had been caught behind the dresser drawer in Annie's kitchen, and I remembered that I'd been wearing my raincoat that day — indeed, it had been such a wet autumn that I'd worn it practically every day.

I went over to the kitchen table and smoothed it out, piecing together the places where it had been torn. It was a sheet of lined paper that might have been torn out of a notebook. There was some writing in ink, slightly smudged in places, but still legible. It was a column of initials. They seemed to be in no sort of order and I stared at the scruffy bit of paper, hoping to make some sort of sense of them. *P.C., F.T., E.T., M.S., W.F., G.P, J.F., M.F., L.C., N.C., T.P., D.P.* What on earth could it mean; was it some sort of code? That was palpably ridiculous. Then I suddenly realized what it was and almost laughed aloud at my stupidity.

"Of course!" I said to Tris, who had been sitting patiently at my feet all this while. "It's the initials of people in the village: Phyllis Craig, Fred Tucker, Ellen Tucker — probably a subscription list or something she was organizing. Oh well, she won't need it now."

I went to throw it away, but some sort of primitive instinct (after all, it *was* Annie's) made me smooth it out and put it carefully away in one of the cookery books on the shelf beside the microwave.

I went into the dining room and began looking at the photos again, but somehow I felt the presence of Annie too strongly. It was an uncomfortable feeling and, on an impulse, I put all the stuff away and went back into the kitchen and made myself a cup of tea. I'd just started to drink it when the phone rang. It was Michael.

"Thea said to ask you if you'd like to come to lunch on Sunday."

"Yes, please, I'd love to. Oh — Michael, I've been meaning to ask you. What will happen to that trust now that Annie Roberts is dead? Will you have to co-op someone else or what?"

"I'm afraid so. If you remember, we are required to have someone from the village."

"Who have you got?"

"A chap called Jim Fletcher, retired bank manager or something — anyway, perfectly suitable."

"But he's an off-comer. Surely it should be someone who's lived there all their life."

"Well, he's agreed now. We've got a meeting next week and this time I think that, without Annie Roberts to egg him on, Brian Norris will vote to wind the thing up."

"What if Jim Fletcher doesn't agree?"

"Oh, he does — we sounded him out before we asked him."

"Michael! That's gerrymandering — is that the word I want? Anyway, it's wicked and probably against the law!"

"Not really. I know you don't approve, but we had to get things sorted."

"So the developers will build the houses and all the money will go out of the village

— it doesn't seem fair."

"Well, as I explained, it will go to help some other charity. Look, I have to go now. See you on Sunday."

My tea had gone cold but I drank it anyway, thinking of Harriet Percy and her good works, and the sepia photograph of the school group in the village, and the young Martha Cross, whose good attendance had earned her a prize, who grew up to be the woman standing on the steps of her cottage in 1954 with a shy young child who had grown up to be Annie Roberts, who had died from a careless mistake.

CHAPTER TEN

The next day I pulled myself together and told myself it was silly to be so obsessed with Annie Roberts. So I went into Taunton and spent a lot of the day making notes on the historical stuff, and, when I got home, I put it on the computer, feeling I'd done a good, professional day's work. Buoyed up by this, the next day I telephoned Father William to see if I could look through the parish records that remained in the church.

"Do come," he said. "I'll be at home all morning."

When I arrived he greeted me warmly. I declined the offer of coffee and, fetching a long woolen scarf, he joined me and we made our way to the church. Our progress through the village was punctuated by greetings and inquiries from various people as to how the Book was going, and when Father William lifted the heavy latch of the church door it was a relief to go into the quiet emptiness of the church. The cold that struck up from the stone floor was scarcely mitigated by the strip of matting that ran the length of the aisle, but fortunately there was an electric heater in the vestry and he switched it on.

"For your benefit," he said. "This garment" — he indicated his cassock — "was designed to keep out the cold of medieval stone floors." He unlocked the cupboard and took out the heavy registers. "There you are," he said, clearing a space at the cluttered table and laying them down. "I see," he continued, as I got out a writing pad and pencil, "that you do not favor the advanced technology."

"I haven't got a laptop," I said, "only a rather ancient sit-up-and-beg computer. No, this is what I'm comfortable with!"

I sat down at the table and drew one of the registers towards me.

"Well, I'll leave you to it. But, please, when you've finished, come and have a glass of sherry — I'm sure you'll need it. Oh, and if you would very kindly switch off the fire and lock the cupboard when you've finished with the registers and bring me the key, that would be splendid." He raised his hand in what might have been an airy wave, or even a blessing. "Good luck to your labors."

I worked steadily for just over an hour and then, feeling a bit stiff (I always work in concentrated bursts), I looked at my watch and decided I'd done enough to justify rewarding myself with a glass of Father William's sherry. I heaved the heavy registers off the table and back into the cupboard, locked it and switched off the fire. Going back into the church, I was startled to come face-to-face with Mary Fletcher, rather strangely wearing a hat and a flowered apron.

"Goodness," she exclaimed, "you did give me a start! I was just coming to get some vases — it's my turn to do the flowers."

"I'm so sorry," I said. "I was in the vestry consulting the parish registers. Father William very kindly gave me permission."

"Oh, I *see* — and did you find anything interesting?"

"There's quite a lot of useful entries I think I can use in the Book," I said.

"Nothing . . . unusual? Well, you never know what you're going to turn up in those primary sources. When I was at the library, one of the staff there was trying to trace his ancestry — so fashionable these days, with all those television programs. He tracked down some parish records and, well, he wished he hadn't!"

"Really?"

"Well, I won't go into details, but you can imagine — he found out several things about some of his relations, grandparents and so forth, that would have been better left alone!"

"Oh dear. No, I found nothing like that."

"Just as well." She sounded disappointed, deprived of a little excitement.

"Well," I said, "I'd better be getting along. I must return this key to Father William."

"I could give it to him if you like."

"No, really, thanks all the same, but I'm passing the vicarage on my way back."

"Well, I'll be getting on, then." She picked up a large bunch of flowers she'd laid down on one of the front pews.

"What splendid dahlias," I said. "Did you grow them yourself?"

"Oh, that's Jim's department — he takes prizes at the Flower Show."

"Well, those would certainly win a prize," I said.

"I can't say I'm fond of dahlias myself," she said. "Always full of earwigs, nasty things. I give the bunch a good shake to get rid of them, but you can be sure there'll always be one left that crawls out when you're arranging them."

I gave her what I hoped was a sympathetic

smile and went on my way.

Since it was a chilly day and since Father William had seemed impervious to cold, I was pleased to see that the firescreen in the grate had been replaced by a real fire and there were sherry glasses and two decanters on the desk.

"Now, do sit down; that is the more comfortable chair. And, please, it's William to my friends." He went over to the desk and turned to look inquiringly. "I can offer you a choice of sherry: fino or amontillado?"

"Oh, amontillado, please," I said. "I know fino is more the thing, but I don't really like it."

He positively beamed at me. "Well-done!" he said. "I have *longed* to hear someone say that!" He poured a glass of the darker sherry. "People are such sheep," he went on as he handed it to me. "If once they're told that something is more 'civilized' or fashionable, they accept it without any reference to their own taste. I have always preferred amontillado myself," he concluded, as if that settled the matter. "Mind you," he said, with the air of one modifying a supposition, "sweet sherry — or *cream* sherry, as it is sometimes called — is quite a different matter."

"Oh, quite," I said. "This is excellent."

"My wine merchant in St. James's sends me down a case. The fino I buy locally." I couldn't help laughing and he looked at me approvingly. "Exactly. It is ridiculous."

We sat for a moment without speaking, peacefully, with our sherry in the warm, elegant room as though there was some unspoken communion between us. William (as I now thought of him) broke the silence.

"Tell me," he said, "did you really want to have anything to do with this book?"

"To be honest I was bullied into it, but, actually, now that I've started, it's really very interesting."

"Bullied by Annie, of course."

"She had a very forceful personality."

"She was an extremely unpleasant woman, in some ways actually evil."

I looked at him. *De mortuis nil nisi bonum?* I suggested.

"Indeed, and one's Christian principles make that mandatory, of course. But just this once I must make an exception."

"I know she was irritating and a bit of a bully, but not evil, surely?"

He got up, went over to the desk and refilled his sherry glass, holding up the decanter inquiringly.

"No, thank you; I'm fine," I said.

He was silent, staring into the fire. Then

he said, "I think I'm going to tell you something I've told no one else. I'm going to tell you, partly because you are writing a book about this village and I think it's something you ought to know, and partly because I have the urge to tell somebody and I think you will understand and, having understood, I'm sure will keep it to yourself."

"Of course," I said.

"Some years ago," he said, "when I was a very young curate in a London parish, my vicar, a man of considerable charisma, was accused of abusing young boys, boys in the choir. Naturally it caused a great scandal and the national papers took it up. He was found guilty and sent to prison — which, indeed, he richly deserved. Unfortunately that sort of mud sticks not only to the perpetrator but also to those around him. You may find it hard to believe, but I had no idea what was going on, but, as I said, I was very young and, in those days, such situations, although they undoubtedly existed, were not widely reported in the media. In the course of the investigation I too came under suspicion and, although I was absolutely cleared, there was a great deal of talk and I was asked, discreetly, if I would consider moving to another parish. I refused, of course, but pressure was put upon me and eventually I agreed. Then, what I feared did happen and there were articles in the local paper saying things like no smoke without fire and so forth. Fortunately it was a nine days' wonder and, when I went to another parish — a pleasant town on the south coast — I was able to put it behind me." He looked at me and smiled wearily. "Of course, it is human nature to believe the worst of people, but it is depressing, shall we say, when it happens to you."

"It must have been horrible," I said.

"In those days, as you will have gathered, I was young and simple, someone it was easy to take advantage of. But I had learned my lesson. I began to build myself another personality. My new parishioners liked their religion spiked up, as they say, so I became Father William and my sermons were more pointed and controversial so that soon I attracted some interest, was asked to write articles, even do a little broadcasting. They liked my new affected manner, so I developed it as you see today. All very camp, and I'm sure everyone thinks I'm gay — I'm not, by the way, but simply that old-fashioned thing: a celibate Anglican priest."

"Omnipresent in Victorian novels," I said, "but not today. Just as there are no bachelors or spinsters anymore; everybody has to be something."

"Very true. You will be wondering," he went on, "why I am burdening you with all this personal history. The fact is that one day, when I had been in Mere Barton for about a year, Annie Roberts let me know, in the subtlest way, that she knew all about that unfortunate period in my past, as she put it. Of course, she said, she wouldn't *dream* of mentioning it to anyone; she quite understood it was better that it should remain buried."

"She blackmailed you!"

"Oh no, nothing as obvious as that. But as time went on I found that she expected me to back her, whenever there were disagreements on the parish council, for instance, or to support any scheme she proposed — that sort of thing."

"And did you?"

"No. I had no intention of submitting to pressure."

"So what happened? What did she do?"

"She came to see me and said how upset she was that I hadn't seen my way to giving her my support on various matters, and she was sure, if I considered it more fully, I would agree that it would make life more harmonious for everyone if I did so. She may have expressed it a little more forcibly, but that was the gist of it."

"Good gracious. So what did you do?"

"I explained, equally forcibly, that on no account would I change my attitude and that if she wished to inform the village of what was a perfectly innocent episode in my past, she was certainly welcome to do so."

"Good for you. Publish and be damned. And did she? Tell everyone?"

"Oh no, bullies very rarely fulfill their threats. She was very wary of me after that, because, you see, I had discovered the secret of her influence over the rest of the village."

"You mean she had a hold over people because of something in their past?"

"Precisely."

"But surely . . ."

"Everyone has something in their past they'd rather other people didn't know about, often something quite small and unimportant — although it seems important to them."

"Yes, you're right," I said thoughtfully. "What an extraordinary thing! But how did she find out all these secrets? I'm sure she was the last person people would confide in."

"She was the district nurse. In and out of people's houses all the time, able to overhear conversations, catch glimpses of papers — many opportunities."

"But that was an appalling betrayal of trust! I see what you mean about evil."

"Precisely."

"I often wondered how she managed to run everything and get support for all her schemes. She didn't want money for her silence. She wanted power; she wanted to run the village!"

"A very big fish in a small pond. A strange ambition, but I believe that when new people — off-comers — came into the village, she and her mother were looked down upon, as I'm sure she would have put it. And she became resentful that these rich newcomers were taking over *her* village and she was being left out. One can understand the resentment, but not the action she took to satisfy it."

"And now she's gone . . . I can see now what you meant, at the funeral, about people being relieved she was no longer able to look over their shoulder."

"I have certainly noticed a certain lightening in the atmosphere."

"Well," I said, "thank you very much for telling me all this." I got to my feet. "Of course, I'll respect your confidence about — well, all of it, really."

"Thank you. And when next you come to look at the parish records, do, please, come and have a glass of amontillado. It is such a pleasure to have a chat with someone outside the village."

When I got home I still hadn't fully taken in what William had told me. The thought that one person could have such influence over so many, and that influence derived from a strange form of blackmail, seemed ridiculous, but then, I could see how it might have happened. Presumably William was the only person who'd the courage to stand up to her. I suddenly thought of Diana's comments at the Harvest Supper. "Thinks she knows everything," Diana had said when she'd had too much to drink. Well, *in vino veritas* — I seemed to be thinking in Latin clichés today — perhaps she had a secret too. Perhaps they all had secrets, large or small, that held them in thrall to Annie. I visualized her as a spider lurking in the middle of a web with flies caught, helpless in the silken threads.

A sudden thought came to me and I went out into the kitchen. The list of initials on that scrap of paper — perhaps that was a list of her victims. I couldn't remember which cookery book I'd put it in so I took them all down, one by one, and shook them to dislodge the loose pieces of paper (recipes from friends, relations, or cut out from magazines) that had been filed away between their leaves. Eventually I found it (in *Food from the Freezer*), smoothed it out once again, and looked at it with new interest.

P.C., F.T, E.T., M.S., W.F., G.P., J.F., M.F., L.C., N.C., T.P., D.P.

Now that I looked more closely, I saw, in a crease in the paper, beside the initials W.F., there was a faint mark — *X* — as though he'd been crossed off the list.

Foss, who had been regarding my activities with the interest he showed in anything I did in the kitchen, leapt onto the work top and began hooking the loose recipes onto the floor, where Tris, attracted by the movement, regarded them with interest. I rescued Annie's list and took it into the sitting room where I sat for some time, staring at it, wondering what, if anything, I should do with it.

CHAPTER ELEVEN

The more I looked at the list of initials, the more confused I became. F.T., E.T., Fred and Ellen — what secret could they possibly have? Or Jim and Mary Fletcher, pillars of rectitude; so were all the others. But as William said, we all have secrets; what would be passed over by the world as not worth considering might be of immense importance to the person involved. The fear of embarrassment should never be underrated. Clever of Annie to use these minor things to manipulate people. But what if there *was* something major? That might be a different matter. I thought of the unlikely book beside her bed; was that part of her scheme?

Something connected with a prominent businessman would surely be major. I resolved to go to the library and order the book straight after lunch.

In the library I got trapped by Anthea.

"What's all this about a book you're writing about Mere Barton?" she demanded.

"It's just a sort of history of the village — there've been a lot of them lately."

"Why are you doing it? You don't live there."

"Annie Roberts asked me to."

"Oh, Annie Roberts," Anthea said dismissively.

"Did you know her?" I asked.

"I've known her off and on for years. When she was a district nurse she used to come and give Mother her insulin injections. A bit of a busybody, I always thought."

"Not a gossip, though."

"No, I will say that for her. She never gossiped, though she must have heard all sorts of things, in and out of people's houses like that."

"She more or less ran that village," I said.

"Oh well, villages." Anthea's voice held more than a hint of scorn. "A lot of old fogys and retired people nowadays. Somebody's got to get things moving or they'd all sit around talking and nothing would *ever* get done." Remembering various meetings at Brunswick Lodge, I smiled inwardly but merely gave a murmur of assent. "No," Anthea continued, "I didn't like the woman — I don't think many people did — but she certainly got things done. We could do with more people like her at Brunswick Lodge."

I shuddered inwardly at the thought of the conflict that would ensue if such a thing was ever allowed to happen.

"Well," Anthea said briskly, "I haven't got all day to stand here chatting. Don't forget to bring that Victoria sponge cake in good time for the coffee morning on Wednesday."

Thinking about it, I decided Anthea was right. I couldn't think of anyone who actually *liked* Annie. I suppose Judith was the nearest thing to a friend that she had, but Judith was always more of a vassal than a friend, and had been rewarded, as vassals sometimes are, with the Welsh dresser. Though, come to think of it, did Annie ever expect her to actually have it? After all, Judith was much the same age, perhaps a little older, so she might not be expected to outlive her. No, I decided Annie had bequeathed the dresser to Judith because it would look good in the will and make it appear that she had a friend.

While I was in the library I thought I might have a look at some of the other village books to see if there was anything there that I might use myself. They all seemed to follow the same pattern, which was useful because it gave me a framework to work to.

I realized that I was becoming absorbed in the project and reflected wryly that I too was dancing to Annie's tune, even though she hadn't had to blackmail me.

When I got home I saw that Foss had been hunting again. The gallbladder of a mouse was laid neatly on the front doormat. This was not a tribute from a grateful pet but merely indicated that Foss had eaten the rest. For some reason he usually chooses to do this at the front door. I am grateful that he no longer goes after rabbits. In the old days visitors used to have to run the gauntlet of a Siamese crouched on the mat, meditatively chewing on a rabbit, starting with the head.

Over my cup of tea I thought again about Annie's list, which I now had safely locked away in my desk. Annie was dead. She couldn't "influence" any of those people ever again. As William had suggested, there must have been a collective sigh of relief when that happened. A persistent thought was nagging away at me; reluctantly, I brought it out into the open and confronted it. Was there, among all those trivial secrets, one so big that the person concerned was prepared to silence Annie? Was her death, in fact, not accidental? Annie and the mushrooms — we all assumed it was an accident. The dark kitchen, the resemblance of the deadly fungus to the harmless variety. But no, that didn't explain it. If Annie had picked those fungi, it would have been in broad daylight; surely an expert like her would have been able to differentiate between them. So someone else had picked the poisonous ones and substituted them for the harmless variety so that in the dark kitchen, etc, etc.

I put the thought from me and got up and began to prepare supper. But cutting up the mushrooms for my omelette brought the whole thing forcibly to mind. I remembered that Annie always left her front door unlocked and, although it was unlikely that anyone with a nefarious purpose would boldly go in that way, it was highly likely that she left the back door unlocked too. I thought of the little gate leading out into the field beyond and wondered whom the field belonged to and if it was easy to get into it unobserved.

Next day I was walking along the village street, looking for the gate that led from the road into the field, when I was joined by Jim Fletcher, who, like Judith and Captain Prosser, seemed to keep up a patrol on the lookout for visitors.

"Hello, Sheila. Can't keep away?"

"I had a few things I wanted to check," I said, "but it's such a nice day, I thought I'd just have a little stroll before I got down to work."

"Well, don't forget, Mary's happy to help. As you know, that sort of thing's right up her street."

"That's very kind and I'll be really glad of her help when I've collected some more material. I'm hoping she'll help me arrange the photos and so forth, and generally help with the layout and the technical side. I believe she said she'd done some sort of course when she was in the library in Farnborough."

"That's right; she did." Jim looked gratified. "She's right up-to-date with all that sort of stuff."

"I expect she misses it," I said. "The library, I mean. Though perhaps you both miss Farnborough — it's quite a wrench to leave somewhere you've lived for some time."

"Oh well, you know, we always wanted to move to the proper country when we retired, and Mary used to come down here — well, Porlock, actually — when she was a child."

"Still, you must have left a lot of friends behind."

"Oh, we're still in touch, you know." He broke off. "Forgive me; there's Judith — I just want a quick word with her. I'll tell Mary what you said."

I continued along the street until I came to a gap between the cottages where there was a gate. I went to look and, leaning over it, I could just see Annie's fence. The gate wasn't padlocked or anything, so it would be easy to go into the field, but I wondered whether that would be remarked upon. There was a path leading diagonally across the field, which was down to grass, and I wondered where it led to and whether there was a right of way. The two horses were still there, but although they turned to watch me, they didn't approach.

"Aren't they lovely! I do like to see horses in a field." It was Judith. "Jim said you were in the village and I wondered how you were getting on."

"They're beautiful horses," I said, ignoring the question. "Who do they belong to?"

"They're Diana's — Thoroughbreds, of course; she knows all about horses."

"Does she own the field?"

"Oh no, it's one of the Tuckers' fields; Diana just rents it."

"And does that path lead up to the woods?"

"That's right. Annie always used to say how convenient it was for her — she could go straight out of her back garden across the field and up into the cover. She used to get all the wood for her fire there and, of course — those mushroom things . . ." Her voice faltered.

"I wondered," I said, "do many people gather them, up there in the wood?"

"A few, sometimes. No one from the village, though; we'd none of us know which ones to pick — not like Annie, who'd been picking them all her life." She sighed. "It just goes to show, doesn't it. I mean, if even someone like that can make a mistake. No, I wouldn't touch them."

She leaned forwards confidentially. "And do you know, I can't even face proper mushrooms now — not after *that*."

"I can quite understand it," I said sympathetically. "It was a shock to everyone, but especially to you, who knew her so well."

"I do like to think I was a special friend," Judith said earnestly. "I couldn't say we were close, exactly — well, you know, Annie always kept herself to herself, as they say, but I think I can say that I knew her better than anybody."

"You've been in the village quite a while now."

"It must be ten, no, eleven years — how time does fly. We came here when Desmond retired. We both fell in love with the cottage but, of course, he didn't have very long to enjoy it, poor soul."

"I'm so sorry."

"Oh well, you carry on, don't you? It would have been easier if we'd had children, I suppose, but that wasn't to be . . ."

"Were you still in touch with your old friends — in Birmingham, wasn't it?"

"That's right. Well, yes, we did stay in touch for a bit, but a lot of them were Desmond's friends — through work and so on — and we didn't have a lot in common. But still," she continued brightly, "I've made lots of friends in the village. I've always been interested in people, and I think that counts for a lot, don't you?"

"I'm sure you're right. I was talking to Jim just now about that and he said they're still in touch with their friends from Farnborough. Do they come and visit?"

"Well, I've never known anyone to come and stay with Jim and Mary — not even their son. Though, of course, they'd only just moved here when he went abroad."

"I didn't realize they had a son."

"Oh yes, Richard — they call him Rick. He went to Australia. Such a good-looking boy. He sent them a lovely photo of himself taken in front of that opera house place in Sydney."

"That was nice."

"They do miss him. I said why don't you fly out there and visit him; you can get quite cheap flights nowadays. But no, Mary won't fly — well, I can't say I blame her. Desmond and I went to Italy one year, to Rome that was, and I swear I held my breath the whole time that plane was in the air!"

I laughed. "I know what you mean. I don't like flying myself. I suppose they might go by boat — there seem to be cruises everywhere nowadays."

"I did think I might go on a cruise myself, after Desmond died, you know, to take my mind off things, but I thought it might be just my luck to be seasick all the time and, from what I've heard, all they seem to do is eat and drink all the time. That wouldn't suit me. I've never taken much of an interest in food — Desmond used to say I didn't eat enough to keep a sparrow alive. Annie, now, she liked her food, always having snacks, picking at things, even though she had three good meals a day. But, do you know, she never put on a pound in weight; some people are like that."

"Well," I said, "I'd better be getting on. I

just want to pop into the shop before I go home."

"I'll walk along with you. I forgot to get my *Radio Times,* though there never seems to be anything I want to watch, all these violent things with people running about in the dark."

The shop was empty and it was Margaret and not Maurice behind the counter. She greeted me brightly, but I thought she was looking tired and not very well.

"I just want some of that smoked eel pâté," I said. "It really is delicious. Oh, and some of the special cheddar I had last time."

"Yes, it's very popular." She leaned forwards and selected a piece of cheese. "Is that about the right size?"

Judith, who had been looking through the magazines, laid her copy of the *Radio Times* on the counter and said, "I'll have a piece of that as well — I do like a bit of bread and cheese for my lunch. So, how are you, Margaret — have you got over that nasty cold?"

Margaret put my purchases in a bag and chose a piece of cheese for Judith before answering. "Yes," she said, "I'm fine now."

"Poor Margaret," Judith said, "went down with this bad cold last week. Such a shame, she was going up to London to see Bridget's show — she's at this art school in London, such a talented girl!"

"Bridget?" I inquired.

"My daughter," Margaret said. "She does theater design; it was the end-of-the-year show and she had several things in it."

"What a disappointment for you," I said. "Was Maurice able to go?"

"He couldn't leave the shop — I wasn't well enough to cope. Still, there's always next year."

A couple of walkers came into the shop, wanting biscuits and asking the way to Lower Barton, so I took the opportunity to say good-bye and go away.

At home I started to make some toast to go with the pâté for my lunch. As I did so I thought about what I'd learned in the village. There was the field, of course, where anyone might have gained access to Annie's back door, but that was not what I found myself considering. Something about the way Jim Fletcher had abruptly broken off our conversation — not his usual style at all — puzzled me. We'd been talking about his friends in Farnborough and he hadn't seemed to want to pursue the subject — again, very unlike him. Usually he'd have kept me talking for ages, giving me the ages and occupations of each and every one. And then, Judith said that none of these friends had ever visited. I suppose there might have been perfectly good reasons for that, though I would have thought he'd have enjoyed showing off their pretty little cottage. No, Jim had been uneasy about something I'd asked and had been anxious to get away. Was there a secret there? Was that the hold Annie had over them? There didn't seem any way I could find out, and really, I had no right to pursue it. Besides, I couldn't imagine that it was the Fletchers who had the major secret that might have put Annie's life in danger.

A smell of burning recalled me to the task in hand and I remembered that my toaster was going through an unreliable phase, either barely coloring the bread or blackening it beyond all use. With a sigh I laid the carbonized slice to one side for the birds (who seemed to enjoy the novel flavor) and put another piece of bread into the toaster, standing over it until it achieved the requisite degree of brownness.

CHAPTER TWELVE

"We haven't had a trip out anywhere for ages," Rosemary said when she phoned. "You've been brooding over that tiresome book and I've been going mad trying to cope with Mother, so I reckon we both deserve a little treat."

A bad damp patch had been discovered in Mrs. Dudley's dining room and the house was invaded by workmen, both within and without. Rosemary's suggestion that her mother might spend a short time in the care home, West Lodge, to avoid the disturbance was instantly dismissed ("I intend to keep a very sharp eye on things here"), which did not stop her from complaining constantly of the inconvenience and discomfort.

"Elsie is a saint," Rosemary said, "and fortunately Mr. Preston has done work for her before and knew what to expect. Anyway, it's finished now, so I haven't got to be in constant attendance, so how about it?"

"That would be marvelous," I said. "Would tomorrow be all right? The forecast's fine, so we might really indulge ourselves and go and have a cream tea at that nice place in Dulverton."

It was a lovely day, mild with mellow sunshine and, along the Exe Valley road, some of the trees had already turned golden.

"It's really good to get right away," I said. "I seem to have been *living* in Mere Barton lately!"

"You certainly seem to be taking this book thing seriously," Rosemary said, skillfully avoiding a pheasant apparently intent on suicide. "I thought you might have abandoned it when Annie died."

"It did cross my mind, but everyone there seemed so keen on the idea that I didn't have the heart to disappoint them. Anyway, I'm sort of interested in it myself now."

"Did you say you'd got some of Annie's stuff for it?"

"Yes. I collected it from the cottage after she died. Actually, while I was in there, I came across something rather odd." And I told her about the list. Of course, I didn't mention William's secret, but I did give her his explanation about how Annie had controlled events in the village.

"Blackmail!" Rosemary exclaimed. "Good heavens. And you think the people on the list all had secrets they wanted to hide."

"It looks like it. You remember that book by her bed, the memoirs of that oil man? That might have been something to do with it."

"How fascinating."

"The thing is," I said tentatively, "something like that might have been a really big secret, too big for whoever was hiding it to let Annie have that sort of hold over them."

"What do you mean? Oh, surely you can't think someone killed her!"

I explained about how I thought Annie wouldn't have made a mistake about the fungi.

"Well, yes, I suppose you could be right about that. But how on earth could someone substitute poisonous ones — always supposing anyone knew enough about the things in the first place."

"It would be easy enough to read up, and, as for getting into the cottage, I'm sure Annie left her back door open, and she was always out and about in the village, so there were plenty of opportunities for someone to sneak in from the field at the bottom of her garden."

Rosemary cautiously overtook a tractor.

"It's all *possible*," she said, "but aren't you just making a mystery where there really isn't one?"

"You're probably right," I said. "It's just that it's been nagging away at me ever since I saw that list."

"Well, I think Father William is right; it was just a way of putting pressure on people — nothing more sinister than that!"

It's never easy to park in Dulverton, even after the holiday season, so we had quite a way to walk to the tearooms we always go to. As we passed another café in the main street I happened to look through the window, and to my surprise I saw Lewis Chapman at one of the tables, in earnest conversation with a young woman. Once we had gone past the café I stopped and told Rosemary what I'd seen.

"Really!"

"I suppose she might have been a colleague," I said doubtfully.

"A *young* woman? And here in Dulverton? I don't think so."

"I suppose not."

"We could go in and have our cream tea there," Rosemary suggested.

"Goodness, no! It would be too embarrassing — that is, if there's anything . . . well, you know . . . Anyway, it's nothing to do with us."

"Perhaps she's Lewis's secret. Was he one of those on Annie's list?"

"Well, yes, he was."

"There you are, then." She turned to look back at the café. "Hang on a minute; they're coming out. Pretend to be looking in this shop window!"

Lewis and the girl stood for a moment outside the café; then he put his arm round her shoulder and they moved off in the other direction.

"Well!" Rosemary said. "Did you see that! Certainly not a colleague. She couldn't be more than twenty, and really pretty."

"Yes. Very pretty. But there could be some perfectly innocent explanation."

"There could," Rosemary agreed, "but I prefer to think the worst."

I can't deny that our cream tea (warm, freshly baked scones, proper strawberry jam and plenty of cream), excellent in itself, had an added dimension as we discussed what we had seen.

"Mind you," Rosemary said as she carefully balanced a strawberry on top of a mound of cream, "you couldn't blame him. I don't imagine life with Naomi is much fun."

"Not a word one would immediately as-

169

sociate with her," I agreed.

"I can't think why he married her, or why she married him, for that matter. It's fairly obvious that her career is the only thing that matters to her."

"And no children," I said. "Presumably she thought they'd get in the way. It's a shame. Lewis is a sweet person; he deserves better. It's that superior manner of hers that always gets to me. No, you couldn't blame Lewis for looking for a little comfort elsewhere."

"I wonder why they were meeting in Dulverton," Rosemary said. "Perhaps she lives down here. We really should have followed them."

I laughed. "I think we're too old to play private detectives," I said. "Anyway, think how awkward it would have been if he'd seen us."

"We've just as much right to be in Dulverton as he has," Rosemary said. "But," she added regretfully, "I do see what you mean. Oh well, you're right; it's Lewis's secret and nothing to do with us."

The next day, when I was thinking about what we'd seen, I decided that however disagreeable it might be for Lewis, if Naomi ever discovered his little affair, it wasn't really a motive for murder. Instead of indulging in profitless speculations, what I really needed to do was finish looking through the parish records.

William gave me the key to the vestry and an invitation to sherry afterwards and I got to work. There wasn't a great deal to be done — much of the stuff had gone to the Records Office in Taunton — and I finished rather too early to present myself at the rectory for sherry. So when I left the church, I went to have another look at the field that ran behind Annie's cottage. I was leaning over the gate trying to work out how easy it would be to slip through unnoticed when I heard a movement behind me. It was Diana, who had dropped one of the two halters she'd been carrying.

"Oh, hello," I said casually. "I was admiring your beautiful horses."

"I never had you down as a horsey type," she said amiably.

I hadn't seen Diana since our encounter at the Harvest Supper and I was relieved to see that she seemed perfectly normal. Indeed, she looked much better than she had for ages, certainly more cheerful. She handed me the halters.

"Here, can you hang on to these while I get the gate open?" It was a metal gate and the fastening was rather stiff. "Damn," she said, "I've broken a fingernail. I must get this latch oiled." She took the halters from me. "Thanks, Sheila. What are you doing in the village anyway?"

I explained about the parish records.

"Oh, that book — are you still going through with it? I thought you weren't too keen."

"I wasn't to begin with," I replied, "but it's sort of grown on me and now I've got quite a lot done it would be a shame to stop. Besides, I feel I owe it to Annie to finish what she started. A sort of memorial to her."

Diana gave a sort of snort of derision. "I don't think we need any reminder of *her*," she said. "Good riddance — and I don't mind who hears me say so — interfering old bat!"

"I know she was a bit hands-on," I said, "more or less running things, but surely she did a lot of good in the village."

"She was far too nosy about things that didn't concern her. In and out of people's houses all the time, eavesdropping on conversations . . ." Then, perhaps thinking she'd said more than she intended, she went on, "I think you'll find I'm not the only one who's glad to be rid of her. Mind you," she added with a short laugh, "I don't suppose they'd come right out and say so!"

She closed the gate behind her. "I must be getting on. The farrier will be here any minute now, and I'm not ready for him."

"Right. I'd better be moving too. Incidentally, is there a right of way across this field?"

She looked at me curiously. "No, there isn't — why do you ask?"

"I just wondered. Judith said Annie used to use it as a shortcut to get into the wood up there."

"Oh, Annie," she said scornfully. "That one was a law unto herself." She gave me a wave of dismissal and went over to the horses.

I looked at my watch and decided it was now a reasonable time to visit William. He greeted me as an old friend, and I decided that since our last meeting we seemed to have progressed from being mere acquaintances to something approaching friendship. Certainly I felt I now knew him very much better and liked him more in consequence. I noticed with amusement that today there was only one decanter of sherry, the amontillado, which seemed to be a little private joke between us.

Today he wasn't wearing his cassock, and in a well-cut gray suit he seemed very much more an ordinary person than a clergyman.

There was the clerical collar, of course, but the small band of white was almost covered by his high-necked pullover. And, what I took to be a further sign of friendship, he had almost completely dropped his usual affected manner.

"So, Sheila, how is it going?"

"I've finished with the parish records now — many thanks — so I can begin organizing the material I've got so far."

"I hope that doesn't mean we won't see you in the village so often."

"Oh no — there's still a lot I need to find out."

"You said 'find out' in a way that makes me think you don't just mean collecting material for the Book. Am I right?"

"Well, yes, in a way," I replied in some confusion.

"All those secrets."

"All those secrets," I echoed, and then I told him about the list.

"And I was crossed out? How gratifying."

"It would seem that you were the only one who actually stood up to her."

"And you want to discover the rest of the secrets?"

"Oh, don't — you make me sound like Annie! No, I was curious, of course, but there's something else. Thinking about it all, I started to wonder if Annie's death *was* an accident, if she knew something so damaging about someone that —"

"That they felt the need to kill her?"

"Well, yes."

"By substituting poisonous fungi for the harmless kind?"

"It would have been possible."

"Poison by fungi — that sounds like something out of Herodotus, or a Jacobean tragedy. It certainly argues a subtlety of mind that I hadn't thought to find in this village. However, you may be right." He clasped his hands together, possibly in thought, possibly in prayer. "Do you intend on telling the police about your theory?"

"I don't think they'd take it very seriously."

"But if you are right, then, perhaps we should."

"We?"

"Like the rest of my clerical brethren, I like a good detective story. So, certainly, anything I can contribute — though within the bounds of my profession, of course."

"The secrets of the confessional?"

"Well, Mere Barton is not yet ready for that, but I do, naturally, hear certain things that I couldn't pass on. But if your natural curiosity leads you to make casual inquiries, perhaps you might like to share your thoughts with me, on a strictly confidential basis."

"It sounds silly, but I do feel that finding that list was in some way *meant,* and if Annie's death wasn't an accident, then perhaps I ought to try to get to the bottom of it."

"Have you made any progress?"

I told him about the book by Annie's bed, but a sort of delicacy stopped me from telling him about Lewis and the girl, perhaps because I felt slightly ashamed of actually spying on them.

"An oil tycoon? That certainly seems strange bedside reading for Annie. I can't, for the moment, think of anyone in the village — certainly not anyone on that list — who might have connections there."

"I've ordered it from the library, so I might get a clue when I've read it."

"Excellent. Now, do have another glass of sherry to fortify you for the task ahead."

We both had another sherry and I said, "There's something I've been meaning to ask you. Who's paying for the publication of this book?"

"Interestingly enough, we have harked back to the eighteenth century — we have subscribers, whose names will be listed at the back, though not, of course, the amount they subscribed."

"That's a good idea. Who organized it? No, don't tell me — Annie!"

"Certainly no one else could have raised quite so much money."

"I can imagine. Will you have enough? Costs go up all the time and now that Annie is no longer with us . . ."

"Actually, I have said that I will be responsible for any shortfall."

"That was very generous of you."

"I rather like the idea of the Book, which is why I was so pleased that you continued with it. And, as it happens, I've recently come into quite a large sum of money — left to me by a distant uncle in Australia, which sounds like a Victorian melodrama, but is perfectly true."

"How lovely," I said appreciatively. "Now I'll feel a particular obligation to do a good job."

As I walked back to my car I met Rachel.

"Hello. I'm so glad I ran into you; I was going to ring you and Rosemary. Phyll and I would like you to come to supper next Tuesday. Martin Stillwell is coming down for a week and we thought it would be nice to have a few people to meet him."

"I'd love to come and I'm sure Rosemary would too. We'll just check the date and ring you. If Martin's coming down, I'll be able to return the key of Annie's — I mean his — cottage. I didn't quite like to trust it to the post."

Driving home, though, I felt reluctant to give up the key. I don't quite know what else I expected to find in the cottage, but I had the feeling that there was still something there that might hold a clue to Annie's death.

CHAPTER THIRTEEN

I'd just come out of a meeting of the Hospital Friends when I saw Lewis Chapman standing by the lift. I greeted him and said, "I'm afraid that one's out of order again."

"I know; Sister Fraser's just told me. Oh well, one of these days we'll get a splendid new Cottage Hospital."

"If they don't close it down altogether!" I said.

"How's the Book going?" he asked.

"Quite well, really. There's still a lot to do, but I've got a nice lot of photographs and Rachel's promised me some of her grandfather going round the village in his pony and trap."

"That sounds fun. Actually, I had been going to dinner there this week (Naomi's away on a course), but I can't because I have to take my daughter to the airport."

"Your daughter?"

"Yes, Joanna, she lives in France with her mother. That's Susan, my first wife."

"Oh," I said, taken aback. "I didn't know . . ."

"We were divorced ages ago. We married far too young and both realized it was a mistake — it was all quite amicable. No, Susan married again and they live in Normandy."

"Do you get to see Joanna often?" I asked.

"Not as often as I'd like, of course, but she's coming over here next year to do her master's degree at Oxford and then it'll be much easier."

"That's nice."

He smiled happily. "She's been down here for a fortnight staying with my sister, Madge, who lives at Dulverton. Poor Madge isn't too well and I was so pleased when Joanna said she'd like to come over and see her." He looked at his watch. "Is that the time? I'd better go and see if the other lift's working — I don't think I can face all those stairs!"

As I walked slowly out of the hospital my first thought was that I was glad I hadn't told William about our "discovery" in Dulverton. My second was delight that Lewis had a daughter, and one who sounded really nice. I remembered with pleasure now how

Lewis had put his arm round her shoulder, a gesture that showed how comfortable and easy they were with each other.

When I got home, of course I rang Rosemary.

"Fancy that!" she said. "And we never knew."

"I suppose there's no reason why we should. Usually we never see Lewis without Naomi and I don't suppose it would crop up in conversation when she's there," I said. "I wonder how she feels about it."

"She's probably dismissed it from her mind as not relevant to her career," Rosemary replied scornfully. "Hang on," she continued. "If that isn't Lewis's 'secret,' does that mean there's something else Annie had on him? Or didn't she know about the first wife either?"

"Well, he doesn't seem to want to hide the fact that he has a daughter if he's told Rachel he's taking her to the airport. And if Annie had got hold of the wrong end of the stick and hinted darkly about a love child, then he'd simply have put her right."

"I suppose so. I wonder if Rachel and Phyll know anything about the first wife," Rosemary said. "Perhaps it will crop up in conversation when we go to supper."

■ ■ ■ ■

It didn't actually crop up, but, soon after we arrived, Rosemary led the conversation round to Lewis, and Rachel said, "We did invite him for this evening, but he had to take his daughter to the airport."

"A daughter?" Rosemary said inquiringly.

"From his first marriage. He married Susan Blakemore — do you remember her? Younger than us — Lydia Blakemore's younger sister. She was in the same form as Phyll."

"Oh yes, I think I remember her, vaguely," I said. "A rather tall girl with red hair."

"Oh, not *red,*" Phyll said. "It was that sort of reddish gold color. She was very pretty."

"They were very young," Rachel said, "and both lots of parents were against it, though they came round in the end. But it wasn't a success. Lewis was still a medical student and there was very little money, and when the baby came it got even worse. She couldn't cope and Lewis was studying all the time, so in the end she went back to her parents and they split up."

"That's very sad," I said.

"I suppose so. But she married a rather nice Frenchman, much older, and now they live in France," Phyll said. "I hear from her sometimes, Christmas and so on. She sounds very happy. She has two sons as well as the daughter from her marriage to Lewis."

"And poor Lewis," Rachel said, "got lumbered with Naomi and no children." She broke off as the doorbell rang. "That will be Martin — he had to go into Taviscombe and see somebody about the will."

She went out to answer the door and I noticed with amusement that Phyll instinctively put up her hand to tidy her hair, and it was noticeable that her eyes lit up when he entered the room. He greeted us with a kind of easy charm and I saw how he would be good at his job, placating difficult tourists and smoothing away any little difficulties.

"Are you down here to see about the cottage?" Rosemary asked. "Are you putting it on the market?"

"No, I don't really want to sell it," he replied. "I'm retiring soon and, as I think I may have said, I'm considering moving down here. Well, when I say retiring, my firm has asked me if I'd consider doing a few trips occasionally, when they need me." He laughed. "It's nice to be asked, and the money will come in handy!"

"It sounds like an excellent arrangement," I said, "and I'm sure you could make the cottage really nice. Annie never really changed anything after her mother died — it's like a sort of time warp! Which reminds me, I must give you back your key."

I felt a strange reluctance to hand it over, but there seemed to be no valid reason for asking to keep it. I felt in my handbag for it and passed it to him.

"I'll need to keep the papers and photos and so forth," I said, "until the Book is published."

"Oh, that's fine," he said. "Keep them as long as you like. As a matter of fact I don't really know what to do with them. That's the difficulty with family things; you can't throw them away, and they're not valuable or unique enough to give to a local museum or anything, and I've no one to pass them on to."

"You have no family, then?" Rosemary asked.

"Alas, no. My wife died two years ago and we had no children."

There was a short silence, a tribute to his bereavement. Then Rachel said briskly, "Shall we go into the dining room? Supper's quite ready."

The food was delicious, and I noticed (as

184

I saw Rosemary did) that Martin poured the wine. He certainly seemed very much at home there and I wondered what Rachel thought about the obvious attraction there seemed to be between him and Phyll. Now that it was established that he was a widower, perhaps something might come of it.

There was the usual conversation about the Book and I gave my usual response about carrying out Annie's wishes, which brought me a sardonic glance from Rosemary.

"She certainly seems to have left her mark on things," Martin said. "Everyone I speak to tells me how much she did in the village."

"You might say that," Rachel said.

There was an awkward silence and I suddenly remembered that Phyll's initials were on Annie's list, and for a moment I wondered what her secret could have been and if Rachel knew how Annie had used it.

"She'll certainly be missed," Phyll said. "Now, who'd like some cheese? There's a Brie and a rather nice local goat's cheese."

"So," Rosemary said when we were on our way home, "what's going on with Phyll and Martin Thing? I thought they'd only met briefly in Madeira. Was it a holiday romance?"

"Hardly," I said. "Phyll was with her father and he was married."

"Well, they certainly seem very cozy now."

"I know — so unlike Phyll, really. She's never been one to make friends easily. I wonder what Rachel thinks?"

"She must be all right about it — I mean, she invited him to stay."

"Or Phyll did."

"Mm. Though I've never known Phyll to do anything like that without asking Rachel. Oh well, good luck to them. Poor old Phyll deserves a bit of luck, after all those years looking after her father."

"Well, she did adore Dr. Craig, so it wasn't exactly a hardship for her. Anyway, it may not be a bit of luck. After all, we don't know anything about Martin."

"We know he's a widower and we know he now owns a cottage — two pluses. Oh, come on, Sheila, she could do with a bit of romance in her life!"

But when I got home I was still uncertain how I felt about Martin Stillwell. There's something about lost heirs turning up out of the blue — all very well in Victorian novels or modern soap operas, but not the stuff of everyday life. I thought again about how Phyll's initials were on that list and I wondered if Annie had suspected there was someone in Phyll's life that had to be kept a secret. Because they were having an affair? Because he was married? And all the time he was Annie's cousin and she didn't know it? That would be a charming irony. And what if he did know about Annie's will and was short of money? What if he seized the opportunity of a chance meeting to ensnare Phyll so that she fell in love with him and killed Annie for his sake? Now, that really was total fantasy. I was allowing my imagination to run right away with me. One step from a mild attraction to a murder!

The animals who had been waiting more or less patiently for their supper decided that enough was enough and my sitting at the kitchen table lost in thought wasn't going to get any tins open. A concerted approach of pleading whines from Tris to peremptory bellows from Foss recalled me to my duty. I was just rinsing out the tins for the salvage when I suddenly said aloud, "Anyway, it couldn't have been Phyll. She and Rachel weren't even in the village when Annie was taken ill!"

"Do you remember Greg Thomas?" Michael asked. "He was at the College of Law with me and came down to stay that summer."

"Yes, of course I do. He was rather nice. Didn't he join a rather grand firm in London — tax specialists or something?"

"That's right. And he was — and still is — nice. So nice, in fact, that he left that practice and went into some sort of community law firm, helping the underprivileged, that sort of thing."

"How splendid."

"He's staying with us for a couple of days — he had to come down to Bristol about a case — and he was asking after you, so I wondered if you'd come to dinner tomorrow."

"That would be lovely. I'll look forward to seeing him again."

Greg Thomas had put on some weight and grown a beard since I last saw him, but he was still the same eager, enthusiastic person I had known and liked.

Conversation was difficult at first because Alice, like a lot of eight-year-old girls, liked to be the center of attention and was, I regret to say, showing off. However, Thea soon scooped her up and took her off to bed on the understanding that I'd go up

188

and read her a story when she'd had her bath.

"Though she reads very well herself," I said, "and quite advanced things. But it's a sort of ritual that I read to her when I come."

"Doting grandmother," Michael observed dispassionately.

"Yes, I know," I said, "but, as they say, grandchildren are your reward for having had children. How about you, Greg? Do you have a family?"

"Yes, Martha — she's my wife — and I have a little girl, Milly. She's five, and there's a boy and a girl, Will and Hannah, both teenagers, from Martha's first marriage."

"Goodness, quite a family. They must keep you busy."

"Oh, it's really good. I came from a large family myself and it's great to have the house full of life. Actually, having teenagers around does help me understand some of the cases I have to deal with at the law center."

"Whereabouts is that?"

"It's in Reading, which I suppose is no more full of problems than anywhere else, though we do seem to have our share. A great deal is drug related so we work a lot

189

with the social services."

"I suppose," I said tentatively, "that it's worse where you get large housing estates and unemployment?"

"That's a lot of it, but we find that more and more young people from middle-class backgrounds are getting involved."

"Oh, the drug thing isn't limited to big cities," Michael said. "We've got it here in Taviscombe."

"Exactly," Greg said. "Well-brought-up young people with loving, caring parents can get involved — a friend of mine had a case a couple of years ago. A nineteen-year-old, good school, university, excellent prospects, went on a gap year to Thailand — you know the sort of thing; they all do it. Got caught up in the drug scene there and formed the habit. Back here he began to deal to pay for his habit and got involved in a drug war and shot someone and is now in prison."

"How dreadful," I said. "His poor parents, what they must have gone through."

"Exactly. Very conventional, highly respected. He was a bank manager and she had some sort of responsible job, and in a quiet town — Farnham, Farnborough, somewhere like that. It was devastating for them. He was their only child. The mother had a nervous breakdown and they felt they had to leave everything behind them and move right away. I don't know what happened to them, but it must have ruined their lives."

Thea came in then and said that Alice was calling for me, but I'm afraid I didn't read very well and Alice complained several times that I was going too fast. But my thoughts weren't on the adventures of the boy wizard and I found it difficult to concentrate. Though when I'd finished the chapter and said good night to my granddaughter, I was reluctant to go downstairs to join the others. The words "bank manager" and "Farnborough" kept echoing through my mind and I had to make quite an effort to pull myself together and contribute naturally to the conversation when I rejoined the others.

It was, of course, ridiculous, I told myself when I got home and could think a bit more coherently. There must be hundreds of cases like that, thousands, probably. And it might just as well have been Farnham and not Farnborough. It would be just too much of a coincidence that this particular case might be about the Fletchers.

I'd put together a sort of rough draft of how the material for the Book might look and in what order it could be presented, so I had, as it happened, a perfectly valid reason for seeing Mary Fletcher to ask for her help. So the next day I arranged to take the draft and some of the material for her to look at.

The Fletchers lived in one of the cottages in the main street, like Annie's from the outside, but inside very different.

"How lovely and warm!" I exclaimed as I stepped from the cold, windy street into the main room.

"We had a wood-burning stove put in," Mary said. "It was dreadfully drafty and miserable before, and it fitted quite well in the old fireplace."

"It looks lovely," I said, moving towards it. "Oh, and you've got the bread oven at the side — how splendid!"

"We tried to keep the original features. Actually, when we were redecorating, we stripped one wall right back and found the old cob wall. If you look over here, we kept a small section of it under glass. There you are — you can see the bits of horsehair."

"Isn't that fascinating! You really have got the best of both worlds — a real feel of the period and all the modern comforts."

"It suits us," she said, "and, of course, I've always been interested in old things. Now, do sit down and I'll go and get the coffee."

When she had left the room I got up and went over to the fireplace. On the mantelpiece above it there were several framed photographs. One of their wedding (both Jim and Mary instantly recognizable in their youthful selves), one of a small boy, about five years old, on a swing, and one that I studied intently, of a young man standing in front of the Sydney Opera House. He was half turned towards the camera, bright-faced and laughing, his hair ruffled by the breeze off the water. A son, indeed, that any mother would be proud of.

When Mary came back into the room I said, "What a nice photo! Is it your son?"

She went over and put the tray with the coffee down on a table.

"Yes, that's Rick — he's living in Australia now."

"Oh yes," I said, gesturing towards the photograph, "the opera house. Does he live in Sydney?"

"Yes. His work is there."

"You must miss him. Have you been out there to visit?"

"No. I'm not very happy flying."

"What a shame. Still, I expect he'll come home to visit you — the young don't seem to be bothered about distances nowadays, do they?"

Although her answers had been quite easy and natural, there was something about the way she was standing, a hint of tension. It seemed unkind to persist, and as I turned away from the fireplace and got out the things I'd brought to show her, I sensed rather than saw that she relaxed.

As I went through the material, I found that she was very competent and was going to be a great help. In that warm, comfortable room, drinking our coffee and discussing practicalities, I felt sympathetically drawn towards her and guilty that I had caused her discomfort, however momentarily.

CHAPTER FOURTEEN

As I drove home it occurred to me that the young man in the photograph had looked *very* young — more like a student, in fact. Perhaps the photograph had been taken when he was on his gap year and he wasn't in Australia at all. Perhaps he *was* the young man in Greg's story — but, really, what did it matter? And even if he was, making sure that particular secret was safe wouldn't be sufficient reason for the Fletchers to kill Annie. I knew now that finding out about Annie's death must be my only excuse for prying into people's lives and I must keep anything I might discover strictly to myself. William had made it plain that he didn't want to know any details, and Rosemary would understand.

Rachel brought round the photographs that she'd promised me.

"I can just remember Davy," she said, pointing to a picture of a sturdy Welsh pony.

"That's him there with the trap. I was allowed to have rides on him, but Mother said
Phyll was too young. Poor Phyll, she used
to be so upset. She always wanted to do
everything I did. I can see her now, hanging
on to the gate of the paddock, watching me
going round on Davy, her face screwed up
trying not to cry!"

"How sad."

"A few years later, Mother decided that it
was the thing for girls to ride so we were
sent off every Saturday to the local riding
stables, but Phyll never got over Davy."

I turned over the rest of the photographs.

"The ones of Higher Barton, when it was
just built, are splendid," I said. "And, oh,
look at this wonderful one of your grandparents having tea on the lawn — goodness,
complete with a maid in a cap and apron
standing in the background!"

"I know. It's like another world — which I
suppose it was. No more maids now —
Filipino couples, I suppose, if you're rich.
Daddy had a sort of housekeeper after
Mother died, before Phyll came home, and
then they had dear old Mrs. Fenn from the
village for a few mornings a week. Now, of
course, we mostly manage by ourselves,
with a little help from Mrs. Bradshaw.
Though it's a big, inconvenient house and

takes a lot of keeping in order. Still, it means that Phyll and I aren't on top of each other."

"So it's working out all right?" I asked.

"By and large, yes. It's not the same, of course, especially for me, but, as life goes on you have to adapt. We're both out quite a bit. This week especially, now that Martin's with us. Phyll's been taking him round all the local beauty spots."

"He's really going to live in the village, then?"

"He seems quite set on it."

"For any particular reason?" I asked.

Rachel laughed. "Because of Phyll, you mean? To be honest I really don't know. I must say I've never known Phyll so *comfortable* with a man before, and he seems to be very relaxed with her. They might be old friends who've known each other for years."

"What does Phyll say?"

"Well, I can't exactly have a heart-to-heart with her while Martin is in the house, and, as I say, they're out together most of the time."

"More than friends? I asked tentatively.

She shrugged. "I think Phyll would like it, but he's so easy and friendly with everyone it's hard to tell."

"Would you mind if they did — you know — get together?"

"Good heavens, no — if that's what she really wanted. Dear old Phyll, she deserves a bit of happiness."

"Do you know anything about him — his family and so on?"

"Not much, without actually cross-questioning him! His wife, Moira, her name was, died, of cancer probably (he hasn't gone into details), but it was a long illness and I think he felt bad about having to be away so often with his job when she was ill. No children, no aged parents — that's about it."

"That and the fact that he's Annie's cousin. I wonder why they never really met."

"I did ask him about that and it seems to have been some sort of family quarrel, generations back, which sounds about right." She looked at her watch. "Goodness, is that the time? I must go."

"Won't you stay to lunch?"

"No, really, I promised Diana I'd have lunch with her — nowhere special, we're only going to the hotel. I think she gets a bit lonely when Toby's away; a bit inclined to hit the bottle when she's on her own. Anyway, I've known them both forever — well, Toby, especially, we were much of an age." She laughed. "Mother always thought he'd be a suitable match for me — you know, son of a gentleman farmer, the nearest thing the village had to a lord of the manor."

"But you never fancied it?"

"Good God, no! A rackety young man; he used to bring a crowd of very dubious people down for the Long Vac when he was at Cambridge, not my cup of tea at all. And I wasn't his! Anyway, he went off to London to work in some rather grand merchant bank — he was never going to be a farmer — and I left to do my training at St. Thomas's, much to Mother's annoyance. She never wanted me to go into nursing."

"Really? What did she want?"

"One of the professions — doctor, lawyer, whatever. Though what she really wanted was for me to marry someone grand, preferably with a title, and do the County thing. I think she thought nursing was rather undignified. But that's what I'd set my heart on. I couldn't wait to get away. Anyway, she bullied Phyll into going to university and then into teaching, so she got her way with one of us. Now I *must* go — we really will do lunch soon."

As I was making my lunch (cheese on toast, hardly lunch at all,) I thought about Toby and Diana, who were also on Annie's list, and wondered about their secret. Of course, Toby was an MP and what might be quite a mild peccadillo in an ordinary person could very well be blown up by the press into something much more. Perhaps he was a Love Rat, or was it the tabloids' favorite word, Sleaze? Either could ruin a career, even though the headlines were based on rumor or spite. Unfair, really. Actually, I always felt there was something slightly uneasy about Toby, a certain defensiveness behind his bonhomie, though perhaps all politicians were like that; perhaps it went with the territory. Certainly he was the one person in the village who might have had most to lose if Annie knew something discreditable about him.

I was suddenly aware of the grill flaring up and I rescued my cheese on toast just in time, though I had to cut the burned bits off round the edges. Alerted by the sudden movements of panic, the animals materialized and demanded their lunch, and I was obliged to put my speculations to one side and cope with my own concerns.

A few days later found me back in the village, ostensibly to have another look at an inscription in the churchyard, but actually to wander around seeing what, if anything, I might pick up. I went into the shop and found Maurice Sanders in earnest conversation with a tall man, whose face looked vaguely familiar.

"I'll let you know, then," Maurice was saying, "as soon as I know anything myself."

He broke off when he saw me come through the door and began putting the man's purchases into a plastic bag. "There you are, then. That'll be £9.20."

The man handed him the money, gave me a brief smile and left the shop.

"Now, then, Sheila," Maurice said, "what can I get you?"

"Have you got any of that Exmoor Blue cheese?" I asked.

"Just had some in. Do you mind waiting while I go out the back and unpack it?"

"No, that's fine."

While I was waiting Judith and Captain Prosser came in and I explained Maurice's absence.

"Oh, that's a lovely cheese," Judith said enthusiastically. "Very expensive, but worth it for a treat!"

"Give me good old cheddar every time," Captain Prosser said. "All this fancy stuff's not a patch on it. A nice lump of cheddar with a bit of home-baked bread and a pickled onion — now, that's a proper way to eat cheese."

"Annie used to like cheddar," Judith said, "and Double Gloucester, and Lancashire for cooking. She never ate soft cheeses; she said they didn't agree with her."

"You must miss her," I said.

"Oh, the village isn't the same without her. We had a parish council meeting last week and really, the ages it took to get everyone to agree to anything — Annie would have had things sorted in no time!"

Captain Prosser looked as if he was about to say something, thought better of it, and sighed.

"People keep arguing all the time," Judith went on, "so nothing gets done. You really need someone strong-minded enough to pull things together. And no one seems to think of good ideas like Annie did. That book of yours, Sheila, that was her idea. How's it getting on?"

"Quite slowly, I'm afraid, but now that Mary is helping, it will be much easier."

"Oh, Mary's so clever," Judith said, "and she knows all about books and things. And, of course, you've got all Annie's photos and papers."

"Papers?" Captain Prosser said. "I didn't know there were papers. What sort of papers would those be, then?"

"Oh, old letters, mostly," I said, "and

some postcards — that sort of thing."

Captain Prosser nodded. "Ah, I see. Interesting."

Maurice came back with the cheese.

"Sheila's just been telling us about Annie's papers," Judith said.

"Papers?" Maurice said.

"Just old letters and so forth," I said. "I haven't quite finished going through everything."

"Anything interesting?" he asked.

"The letters from Annie's grandfather when he was in France in the First World War," I said. "They're very moving. And accounts of village festivities — cuttings from the local papers, all quite long ago."

"Nothing more recent, then?"

"Not really, though, as I said, I haven't been through everything yet."

"Have you got all the material you need for the Book, then?" Judith asked.

"More or less," I said, "though Diana did say there were some things, photos and so forth, from Toby's family."

"They should be fascinating," Judith said. "After all, they've lived in the village for generations!"

"Yes, I really must get onto her about them."

"How much of this cheese do you want?"

Maurice asked.

"Oh, that piece will do nicely. Oh yes, and a couple of slices of that ham."

When I left the shop I walked along to the field where Diana kept her horses, but there was no sign of her and I didn't feel like making a special journey up to the house, so I decided I'd ring her instead. I stood for a moment, leaning on the gate, watching the horses moving slowly across the field, cropping the grass as they went. As I was watching, I saw a figure coming out of the wood and taking the path across the field. It was Margaret Sanders. She greeted me as she got to the gate.

"Hello, Sheila, you looked lost in thought."

"I was just admiring Diana's horses."

She put down the bundle of branches she was carrying and tugged at the fastening of the gate. I gave it a push to help her open it.

"Thanks. It's a bit stiff; I think it needs oiling."

"Have you been for a walk?" I asked.

"I've been up in the wood to get some beech leaves," she said, picking up the bundle. "I'm doing a demonstration for the WI about how to preserve them in glycerine."

"How lovely. I always keep meaning to do that myself, but I never seem to get around to it. You seem to have got a splendid lot. Are there a lot of beech trees up in that part of the wood? I don't think I've ever been up there."

"Quite a few."

"I believe beechwoods are good for finding fungi, something to do with an open canopy."

She shook her head. "I don't know. I've never fancied them," she said. "You really want to know what you're doing and I couldn't be bothered, reading it all up."

"And even if you do know what you're doing," I said, "you can still make a mistake — like poor Annie."

"Oh well, Annie had to know best about a lot of things, and look where it got her."

I nodded agreement. For something to say I asked after her daughter at art school.

There was an imperceptible pause before she said, "Bridget? Oh, she's doing very well."

"Such a pity you couldn't get to her exhibition. Whereabouts was it?"

"Oh, it was just at the school, nothing very grand."

"Still, it would have been nice for you to have gone."

"There'll be another time." She moved the bundle of branches more securely under her arm. "I'd better be getting along and start on these. Nice to have seen you."

I watched her walking back to the shop and wondered if something about their daughter — it really had been a hesitation — was the secret that Annie held over them. We are at our most vulnerable where our children are concerned.

I was still standing by the gate when Judith came by.

"Hello," she said. "Were you looking for Diana?"

"I thought she might be here, but I'll leave it for now."

"Come to think of it, she might be in London. She usually goes up when there's some political thing of Toby's."

"I'm surprised she's down here most of the time. I mean, she is a politician's wife, and he has a London constituency after all, and there must be things there she has to go to."

"I know," Judith said. "I often think it must be difficult for Toby sometimes — but, of course, he's so devoted to her." She lowered her voice. "I did hear that she only agreed to marry him if she didn't have to be up in London all the time, and he was so keen that he agreed. Such a charming man — I do think he deserves a little more support." She leaned towards me and spoke even more quietly. "They do say that she is a little fond of the bottle. I don't know if you saw how she was at the Harvest Supper. Of course," she went on in a more normal voice, "she has the money. Her father was a Member of Parliament, but very rich — a millionaire — and she was his only daughter."

"Really?"

"Oh yes. I remember seeing the photos of the wedding in the paper — that was before we came to live here — very grand, St. Margaret's Westminster. She made a lovely bride."

"How interesting. She certainly has some beautiful horses. I've been admiring them. Actually," I said, turning towards the gate, "I hadn't realized that path across the field was a right of way."

"It isn't really, but everyone uses it to get to the wood. It's all right as long as people are good about keeping the gate shut."

"I've just seen Margaret — she told me she was up there getting beech leaves for a demonstration for the WI."

"That's right. She's the president now that Annie's no longer with us."

"I was asking her about her daughter — the one at art school. She sounds very talented."

"Margaret's ever so proud of her. It was such a pity she couldn't get to the exhibition."

"I expect they see her in the holidays when she comes down here."

"She used to, but these last two holidays she's been abroad — something to do with her art school, I think. It's a shame, really; they're such a close family."

Later that afternoon I was just about to go into the library when I saw Michael coming out of his office a few doors away. He was with the man I'd seen talking to Maurice in the village shop earlier on. The man got into his car and drove away and Michael turned and saw me.

"Oh good," he said. "I was going to phone you. Thea said could you possibly meet Alice from school tomorrow — her car's acting up — and come back to tea with her."

"Of course, I'd love to. I'll give Thea a ring — I've got some frozen raspberries she might like to have." I hesitated for a moment. "Michael, who was the man you were just with? I'm sure I know his face, but, for the life of me, I can't think of his name."

"Oh, that's Bob Carver. It's his firm that's buying the field from the Percy Trust."

CHAPTER FIFTEEN

Of course, I thought as I went into the library, there may be no sinister reason for Bob Carver to have been in the village shop talking to Maurice. For all I knew he might live in or near Mere Barton and had every right to be in the village shop. I made a mental note to try to look him up in the telephone directory when I got home. I skirted round the tables of computers, which seem to take up more and more space these days, and made for the Biography section, where I found Rosemary.

"Hello," I said. "You look harassed. Is anything the matter?"

"Just Mother as usual. She's had a bad cold that's gone on to her chest."

"I'm sorry. Is she all right?"

"It's not serious, but Dr. Macdonald says she mustn't go out, so she's getting bored. I'm trying to find something to keep her occupied." She held up a book. "Do you think she'd like this life of Florence Nightingale?"

"It looks a bit heavy," I said, "in both senses of the word. Tiring to hold up if she's in bed."

"You're right, of course. Why must people write such *enormous* books? Oh well, it'll have to be another Dick Francis if I can find one. Such a blessing when there's racing on television — that and the antiques programs!"

"Would she like a visit?" I asked.

"That would be angelic of you, if you can bear it. Tomorrow morning for coffee — she has a rest in the afternoons now, I'm glad to say. It gives Elsie a bit of a break."

Elsie has been with Mrs. Dudley for many years now and is devoted to her and rather proud of what she calls her whims and ways. She greeted me cheerfully when I called the next day.

"She's feeling much better today," she said. "She really brightened up when she knew you were coming and insisted on coming downstairs."

Mrs. Dudley was, indeed, downstairs, and looking very much her old self.

"Good morning, Sheila," she said. "I must apologize for all this." She indicated her dressing gown (blue, and of the finest Pyrenean wool) and slippers. "But Dr. Macdonald, who is a silly old fool, insists that I spend most of the day in bed."

"I'm so sorry you've been ill," I said, as I handed her the bottle of cologne I had brought, despairing of finding flowers she might find acceptable.

She looked at it critically and then gave me a nod of approval. "Thank you, Sheila — most thoughtful of you."

Elsie brought in the tray and my heart sank when I saw the delicate china coffeepot. Not as heavy as the silver teapot that always caused me such anxiety, but of an elegance and fragility that always made me feel instantly clumsy and sure I was going to break off the exquisite curved spout. Elsie gave me a reassuring smile and poured the coffee herself before she went away and in my relief I took two pieces of her heavenly shortbread. Mrs. Dudley put me through the usual cross-examination about my life and activities and those of the family, but that was merely the preliminary before we got down to the news and gossip.

"So," she said, brushing a few crumbs from the Pyrenean wool, "how are you getting on with that *book?*" She gave the word a complex emphasis, implying interest, disapproval and a general feeling that I was, yet again, wasting my time on something unworthy.

"Oh," I said hastily, hoping to divert her attention to some less controversial subject, "it's coming along."

"Of course, Mere Barton isn't a proper village anymore," she said. "Full of retired off-comers. I don't see how you can find anything to write about."

"It's really a sort of history and there's still a few families left who've been very helpful, looking out photos and things — the Tuckers at the farm and Toby Parker and Phyll Gregory and Rachel, too, now she's back again — memories, you know, of how things were."

"Oral tradition," Mrs. Dudley said. "They're always going on about it on the wireless."

"Well, yes, I suppose you could call it that."

"Asking people to send in stories about the past. I would have thought most of that would be better forgotten. *I* believe in living in the present."

Since Mrs. Dudley spent most of her time asserting how much better things were in the old days, this barefaced volte-face indicated that she'd taken up her favored attitude, that of the opposition.

"Ellen Tucker has lots of marvelous photos," I said enthusiastically. "Some lovely ones of work on the farm — splendid old carts and horses, and some of the village schoolchildren and the bell ringers' outings — really fascinating." Mrs. Dudley looked unconvinced. "And," I went on, "Phyll has some beautiful ones of the house, Higher Barton, when it was first built and lovely Edwardian tea parties on the lawn."

"Oh well, of course," Mrs. Dudley said, instantly rejecting her passion for the present, "people knew how to do things in those days. They knew the proper way to go on. You will scarcely credit it, Sheila, but the other day when I was at the hairdresser (they usually come to me, but there was some sort of difficulty, most inconvenient) the girl offered me coffee in a *mug!*"

"Goodness," I said inadequately. "How perfectly dreadful," I added, feeling that something more was required by the enormity of the offense.

Mrs. Dudley nodded. "You may well say so. I said to the girl, 'Do I look like the sort of person who would drink out of one of those things?' Of course Brooke — she's a nice girl; she understands my hair — was very apologetic and fetched my coffee in a proper cup. But, really, *Brooke.* What sort of name is that for a girl!"

"I know," I said. "I came across a girl on the television called Tayler the other day."

"Oh well, television," Mrs. Dudley said dismissively. "Did you say Toby Parker was helping you with this book? I would have thought he had enough to do looking after his constituents, though I wouldn't care to have him for *my* MP. He was very wild as a young man — I know his father was very worried about him at one time. I believe he thought of sending him off to his cousin in Canada, but Toby wouldn't go, so they got him a job in the city (some sort of merchant bank), and the next thing I heard he was in Parliament. Influence, of course, typical of that family. And by then he'd married Diana Francis and it was her father's old seat that Toby got, so you see . . ." She took a finger of shortbread and broke it into smaller pieces. "That's the way things go. And MPs are never in Parliament anyway. When you see them making speeches, there are all those empty seats!" She bit into the shortbread.

"Actually," I said, "it's Diana who's looking out the photos for me."

"How is she?" Mrs. Dudley demanded. "I hear she's been drinking again. You remember she had to go to that place a while back to be — what do they call it? — dried out."

I didn't feel able to go into Diana's drinking habits so I just said, "She was fine when I saw her a little while ago."

"Her uncle died of drink — liver failure, though they called it something else. It's in the family."

"She said there's a whole lot of photos in a trunk somewhere," I said, ignoring this little piece of family scandal. "I'm hoping she'll look them out when she gets back from London. Time is getting on. The text's more or less done and I'd like to get the captions for the illustrations finished. I've done Phyll's and those from the Tuckers — oh yes, and the ones Annie Roberts gave me before she died."

"Annie Roberts," Mrs. Dudley echoed. "Now, that was a most peculiar affair."

"In what way peculiar?"

"Mushroom poisoning. I thought she was supposed to be an expert."

"Well, apparently it's easy to mistake the poisonous ones from the ones that aren't, and it's very dark in her kitchen. She was quite ill for several days but no one thought it was serious until she collapsed and Lewis Chapman sent for an ambulance."

"Lewis?" Mrs. Dudley's tone softened.

"Such a nice young man, so understanding and sympathetic when I had the anesthetic for my leg. A real gentleman, unlike some members of the medical profession these days, seeing patients in open-necked shirts. No, Lewis is one of the old school. Such a pity about that first marriage — I said at the time it was a mistake, both of them far too young, and then with that child!"

"She seems to have grown up into a nice young woman," I said, "and very fond of her father."

"Where did you see her?" Mrs. Dudley demanded sharply.

"Oh. Just casually, in passing," I replied vaguely, remembering the circumstances. Though I daresay Mrs. Dudley would have approved of our undercover activities.

"And then," she went on, "when he was free of that entanglement, Naomi Cromer got her claws into him."

"I must admit," I said, "I've never really warmed to Naomi; she always seems so cold and hard."

"Exactly." Mrs. Dudley nodded emphatically. "Just like her mother. She was one of the Harrisons — I knew her quite well at one time; we were on several committees together — they always thought very well of themselves, though *her* father was only a

217

shopkeeper, in quite a small way."

"Really?"

"Oh yes, but they certainly gave themselves airs, so it was very difficult for them when Naomi was involved in that scandal."

"Scandal? What sort of scandal?"

"Oh, something medical," she said airily. "I never heard the ins and outs of it — all hushed up, of course. But Dr. Denver — he was my doctor before Dr. Macdonald, one of the old school — told me about it. It seems there was some sort of research, up in London at one of those teaching hospitals, where it turned out that some of the facts, or figures or something, had been falsified."

"Goodness! And Naomi was part of the team?"

"Exactly. That's why she had to come down here. Such a disappointment for her family," Mrs. Dudley added with relish, "after they'd gone on about how brilliant she was, all set for the Nobel Prize! Of course, they said it was due to ill health; well, what else could they say? That's why she made a dead set at poor Lewis."

"At a time when he was feeling vulnerable," I said. "Do you think he knew? About the scandal, I mean."

"I suppose she'd have had to tell him.

Probably *after* they were married!"

"Poor Lewis. Well, I hope this nice grown-up daughter will be a comfort to him."

"If Naomi lets him see her."

"Oh surely —"

"I wouldn't put anything past that woman," Mrs. Dudley said firmly. She drank the last of her coffee and I took this as a signal for my dismissal.

As I kissed her good-bye she felt very frail and I suddenly realized how time had passed. When I'm with her I'm so used to feeling a mere schoolgirl, Rosemary's friend, but now (it suddenly swept over me), I'm in late middle age and she is old. One day in the not too distant future she won't be here anymore, and in a little while after that, neither will I.

I took my gloomy thoughts down to the sea wall, my favorite brooding place. Now that the summer visitors were gone, the council had stopped smearing the rails with whatever it was they put on them to keep the seagulls away and, to my delight, they were back again, a row of little terns, with the odd gannet and herring gull swooping overhead. As I got out of the car other gulls on the beach flew up, hoping to be fed, but today I had nothing for them. I walked along for a little way, and stood watching a container ship moving slowly up the far side of the Bristol Channel to one of the Welsh ports. As I turned to go back to the car I saw a figure approaching. Somehow I wasn't surprised to see that it was Lewis Chapman.

"Not a very nice day," he said as I approached, "but after a tiresome committee meeting at the hospital I felt the need of a little fresh air. How about you?"

"Not a committee meeting," I said, "but I just felt a bit depressed and somehow all this" — I made a vague gesture — "helps. It's soothing, I suppose."

He smiled. "It works for me."

"How is Naomi?" I asked.

He looked surprised, as well he might, since I don't usually inquire for her when we meet. "She is fine — very busy, as usual."

"Oh, good. It's just that I thought she looked a bit tired when I last saw her," I improvised hastily.

"Oh well, she's just started a new project, so, as I said, it's a busy time for her."

"Of course."

"So how's the famous Book coming along? We're all looking forward to it in the village."

"Oh, I'm making quite good progress.

People are being very helpful. But it's so sad, that poor Annie won't be here to see it."

"Yes, poor Annie," he echoed, somewhat perfunctorily, I thought.

"Such an unnecessary death," I said, "especially as she'd been eating those fungi perfectly happily for years."

"Well, I suppose people get overconfident . . ." His voice trailed off. "Oh well," he said, "I suppose I'd better be getting back. Nice to have seen you, Sheila, and good luck with the Book."

Watching him hurrying away, I was left with the feeling that he wasn't keen to talk about Annie, and I wondered whether it was because she'd known why Naomi had left her research job in London. If Dr. Denver knew about it — and he was a tremendous old gossip — then it was almost certain that Annie did too. And that would have been the hold she had over them. But surely that wouldn't have been enough motive for murder.

They were mounting up now, all the secrets Annie could have known. William was right; we all have things we'd rather people didn't know about. Not necessarily bad things or illegal things, sometimes just embarrassing, but things we wish to keep to ourselves. Things, indeed, that we've tucked away at the backs of our minds and had hoped to have forgotten. Small things but powerful if used as subtly as Annie had used them.

Rosemary rang me that evening to thank me for visiting her mother.

"I hope it wasn't too much for her," I said. "I wasn't sure if she should be downstairs."

"Oh no, it did her a lot of good. You know Mother; stimulation is what really helps and I gather she was able to fill you in on a fair bit of gossip?"

"As always," I said, and told her about Naomi.

"Yes, I do vaguely recall Mother telling me about it, ages ago. She had several run-ins with Mrs. Cromer on various committees, so it was manna from heaven to find out that her precious daughter wasn't as clever as all that. No, I had the whole saga all over again this afternoon — Mother hasn't been so animated for days!"

I laughed. "She certainly did seem to gather momentum as the story went on."

"Anyway," Rosemary said, "now that she's been downstairs once, she thinks she can get up tomorrow and watch the racing on the television in the sitting room. She says the one in her room makes people look funny."

I laughed. "It really is extraordinary, your mother's passion for racing. Does she ever have a bet?"

"Goodness, no. She might lose, and Mother would hate to lose at anything! Anyway, she doesn't think the Queen bets."

"Not even on her own horses?"

"We don't go into that."

"I suppose that stuff about Naomi was the hold Annie had over her and Lewis," I said.

"Sure to have been. I daresay she knew a lot of medical secrets."

"Not just medical, really. As a district nurse she'd be in and out of people's houses all the time. People might have confided in her, trusted her — patient confidentiality, you know, like a doctor."

"Using that sort of thing would have been a terrible betrayal of trust," Rosemary said. "Do you think she was really that bad?"

"It looks like it."

"How do you know —" she began, then stopped and said, "No, don't tell me. If you've found out things, *they'd* be secrets and I don't think I ought to know."

When Rosemary had rung off I made myself a cup of hot chocolate, fed the animals and went to bed early, trying to lose myself in the quiet pleasures of *The Provincial Lady,* reflecting that life in E. M. Delafield's village, full of incident though it was, was a good deal more comfortable than life in Mere Barton.

CHAPTER SIXTEEN

The library sent me a card to say that the
book I ordered was now in and so I went to
fetch it. Looking at the photograph on the
cover I wondered again what had made Annie — notoriously careful with money —
willing to pay what she would have considered a sizable sum for such a book. I put it
in my bag and went on to do my shopping.
It was a chilly day (autumn was really upon
us) and dodging the blustery showers was
tiring, so when I'd finished I felt I deserved
a coffee and made my way to the Buttery. It
wasn't too crowded and I was just making
for a seat where I could have a look at the
book when I saw Phyll beckoning me over
to where she and Martin were sitting.

"Hello, Sheila, lovely to see you," she said.
"Come and join us." She looked excited,
like a child who's just been told of a pro-
jected treat. "Isn't it splendid? Martin's
definitely coming to live in the village!"

"Really?" I said. "That's" — I searched for a suitable word — "absolutely *splendid.*"

"Well," Martin said, "I've more or less retired and, since I don't want to sell the cottage, it seems silly to keep the flat on as well. I can do any trips I have to do just as well from Mere Barton as from London."

"Of course."

I wondered if he would feel any regret at leaving a place where he had lived for many years with his late wife, if there might be memories — unhappy ones, perhaps. Maybe that was why he wanted to get away. And, of course, there was Phyll. He must surely know by now how she felt about him. Just now, leaning eagerly across the table, her eyes shining, it was very obvious how happy this move had made her. I caught Martin's eye and he gave me a half smile as if he had read my thoughts, so I said hastily, "Will you like being part of village life, do you think?"

"Oh, I hope to fit in. The people there seem very friendly."

"You'll have to do quite a bit to the cottage," I said. "I don't think Annie had much done since her mother died."

"Oh yes," Phyll broke in, "it's so exciting. We've been and had a good look round. The whole place needs doing up — decorating and so forth — and it really does need a new kitchen and bathroom!"

I wondered how Martin felt about the way Phyll seemed to be taking over the whole project. He smiled again — it was a warm, friendly smile that reassured me that he really did care for her.

"Phyll's been an enormous help," he said. "Lots of marvelous ideas for doing it up. I'm most grateful!"

"It's not the best time for selling your flat," I said.

"Oh well, I haven't got to buy anything, so I can afford to take a lower price. Really, I just want to move as soon as I can."

"Certainly you wouldn't want to leave the cottage empty for too long," I said. "It seemed to me when we went in it that everything was very damp."

"I know," Phyll said. "It was really bad. So I lent Martin a couple of our electric heaters to warm things up — they'll do until he can get some proper heating arrangement. Annie had open fires and *nothing* upstairs — imagine! — but I think a wood-burning stove in the sitting room would be nice. That could warm the whole house and give you hot water as well."

"A splendid idea," Martin said. "I'll see what I can find online."

"Oh, don't bother," Phyll said. "I'll look out some brochures we had from Jack Cartwright — he's our builder — Father and I got them when we thought of having one at Higher Barton."

"I suppose I'll have to get things moving pretty soon," Martin said, "or winter will be upon us and the bad weather might hold things up. Perhaps I'd better have a chat with this Jack Cartwright of yours."

I left them making plans and went home wondering just how far Martin had committed himself as far as Phyll was concerned and what Rachel thought of the whole affair. If Phyll got married (and it looked as if things might be heading that way), then Rachel would be alone in that big house and she might wonder if moving down from Inverness was a good idea after all.

Maddeningly, the animals were particularly demanding when I got home and it was a little while before I could really settle down and look at the book. I opened it first at the index, looking for familiar names and, sure enough, there was an entry for Toby Parker. But it was disappointing. He was mentioned only as a member of a parliamentary committee, something to do with balance of trade and imports, quite complicated. I'd have to ask Michael to explain it.

There was no other name in the index that had a connection with anyone in the village. Still, at least Max Holtby had mentioned Toby by name; he knew who he was.

Perhaps Annie had heard — or overheard — something that had aroused her suspicions about Toby's financial activities and had prompted her to spend good money on the book. But, equally obviously, it occurred to me there wouldn't be anything in the book that overtly connected Toby with Max Holtby in any inappropriate way. If there'd been just a hint of that, even though Toby was a very minor backbencher, the press would have been onto it at once and the usual Sleaze headlines would have been trotted out.

I skimmed through the book while I had my lunch. A rags-to-riches story — impoverished Scottish childhood, widowed mother, scholarships to a good school and then to Oxford, geological expeditions in the Middle East, taken on by an oil company, headhunted by a major oil company, useful Middle East connections leading to membership of the board and then managing director — a brilliant career, helped by sharp decision making and general ruthlessness, an eye for the main chance. The sort of person, perhaps, who would know how to buy influence if he felt it necessary.

I looked again at the picture on the jacket. Yes, certainly that sort of person, someone who was used to getting his own way. And he knew Toby's name. A few discreet inquiries about Toby's personality — would he be persuaded, by bribery or flattery, or a combination of the two, to "be helpful" in putting a certain point of view, a word, in the right place. From what I knew of Toby (weak and open to flattery), all this was quite possible.

So, if Annie had any suspicion that all this was going on, it would give her a very positive hold over him. Nothing overt, of course, but sarcastic comments and intimations that she knew . . . what? I remembered several exchanges between them; he was certainly uneasy with her. Of all the people in the village that Annie was blackmailing, he had the most to lose.

Had Toby been in the village just before Annie died? I didn't think so. He was certainly at her funeral and, now that I came to think about it, was most anxious to know what would happen to the contents of her cottage — perhaps worried that she'd committed something incriminating to paper. But although he hadn't been in Mere Barton when she was taken ill, Diana was.

The more I thought about it, the more I saw how easily Diana could have (quite naturally) walked across the field and, having made sure Annie was out, preferably at a meeting that would take some time, slipped into the cottage by the back door and substituted the poisonous fungi for the harmless ones. She adored Toby, would have done anything for him. Diana made no secret of the fact that she loathed Annie, probably because of the way she'd been tormenting Toby about his secret. I wondered if he'd put her up to it (thus giving himself an alibi), or if she'd thought it out herself and Toby had no idea. Either way, the stress of it all would account for her drinking and general fragility. I sat for some time considering all this and was startled to realize that it was after three o'clock and I was still sitting there with the remains of lunch and the unwashed dishes all around me.

The next day I was back in Mere Barton again, having decided to call on Diana with the perfectly valid excuse of asking for Toby's old family photos. Amazingly, the village street was empty for once and I arrived at the farmhouse without being waylaid by anyone. To my surprise the door was opened by Toby himself.

"Hello," I said. "I'd no idea you were down here."

"Parliament's still in recess," he said, "and I felt the need for a little rest and recuperation after a particularly tiring round of constituency affairs. Anyway, how can I help you, unless it's Diana you want. I think she's out with the horses."

"No, actually, it's you I really wanted to see."

"Oh, right, come on in, then." He led me through the dark-paneled hall. "Do you mind coming into the study? I need to save some stuff on my computer. I was just trying to write something for the *Telegraph* — not my sort of thing at all, really, but you have to make the effort." He pressed a few keys and turned to face me. "There; that's it."

He waved me to a chair and sat down at his desk. "Now, then, what can I do for you?"

I explained about the photographs. "And, actually," I said, "I've got the first draft of the Book done and I left a space for them, so I'd be most grateful if you could let me have them — well, now, if possible. Diana was going to look them out, but I expect she forgot."

"Ah, the photos."

"They'd really contribute so much," I said. "I think Diana said something about them being in a suitcase in the barn . . ."

"No." He got to his feet and went over to a cupboard. "They're here. After you mentioned them I thought I'd like to look at them myself, so I went and rescued them. I thought I'd like to have a look at my younger self!" He gave an embarrassed grin. "It's odd to think that forty years can turn your early life into actual history." Toby took a cardboard shoe box out of the cupboard and tipped the contents out onto the desk. "Come and have a look."

He picked a photo out at random and looked at it. "Hardly Brideshead," he said, "but it seems just as unreal."

It was a picture of a group of young people on a tennis court. The young men wore long white flannels and the girls knee-length white tennis frocks. It wasn't only the old-fashioned hairstyles and tennis racquets that spoke of time past; it was the whole atmosphere. I remembered a scene in a repeat of an old black-and-white television program — a roomful of young people, most of the boys in jackets and ties, the girls with beehive hairdos, doing the twist. There were no flashing lights, no heavy beat, no obvious drink, even, only a gathering of youngsters enjoying themselves in a completely uncomplicated way.

As if he had caught my thoughts, Toby said, "Life was simpler then. All right, we weren't angels by any means, but things weren't so — so full-on." He picked up the photo and looked at it again. "The tennis court went years ago — I'd forgotten all about it. We used to have tennis parties — homemade lemonade, can you believe it . . ." His voice trailed away.

"I remember tennis parties," I said, "and the lemonade."

"I brought a couple of chaps down here for the Long Vac." He indicated a tall, good-looking young man in the middle of the group. "That's Evan Fraser. He was up at Trinity with me, went into the army, died in the Gulf War. I'd forgotten him too." He bundled the photographs back into the box and pushed it towards me. "Here, you take them and sort out what you want. There's a lot of really old ones you might be able to use."

"Thank you," I said. "I'll let you have them back as soon as I can."

"No hurry. I don't particularly want to look at them again." He put the lid back on the box and said, "Will you have a drink?"

"Well," I said, "it's a bit early . . ."

"Oh, come on, Sheila — I could do with one and I can't drink alone. What'll it be? Whiskey or sherry?"

"A sherry would be nice," I said.

He poured a sherry for me and a large whiskey for himself.

"Stupid to let things get to you," he said.

"Old photos will do it every time," I said.

This was a Toby I'd never seen before, perhaps the real Toby, shaken out of his public persona by a jolt into his past.

"So you've nearly finished this book, then?" he said.

"More or less. Mary Fletcher's been a great help and so has Father William, and lots of people in the village have looked out stuff. I really need to get it done as soon as possible because I've got quite a bit of my own work piling up. I only took it on because Annie more or less forced me into it."

"Oh Annie — she was very good at forcing people to do things." His voice was harsh.

"So I gather. It seemed to me that she had some kind of hold over several people in the village."

"You could say that."

"Over you?" I asked.

He looked at me sharply. "What made you say that?"

"She had a copy of Max Holtby's memoirs beside her bed."

"There's nothing in that."

"True, but she'd actually gone to the trouble of buying a copy . . ." I let my voice trail away.

Toby got up abruptly and poured himself another whiskey. "You've been through her papers, haven't you? Was there anything . . . anything about me?"

"Not that I've found," I said. "So far."

He put his glass down on the desk and leaned towards me. "Look, Sheila. I don't know what the old hag heard or thought she heard — she was always about the house when Diana had that septic leg and I sometimes took phone calls in the hall when she was passing through. And yes, I had some calls from Max. Come to think of it, she once took a message for me from his secretary when Diana was laid up and couldn't get to the phone. And, yes, I did tread a pretty fine line sometimes, but I swear I never did anything illegal."

"But there were things you wouldn't have liked the press to know about, for instance."

He shook his head. "It's a bloody mine-field, politics, these days. I'm standing down at the next election — that's confidential, mind. I've had enough. It's a young man's game nowadays, anyway."

"What will you do?" I asked. "Come down here?"

"I need to for Diana's sake. What's it they usually say? — 'spend more time with my family' — well, in my case it's true. You know how Diana's been. Ever since that bloody woman started . . . It's been a bit better since she died, thank God, but Diana does need me around to keep her steady. We can make out all right. I'll have my pension, Diana's got some money of her own and I've got a bit put by." He glanced at me sharply. "All perfectly legal."

"Of course," I said.

"It'd have been different if we'd had children," he said. "Horses aren't really a substitute."

"No."

He picked up his empty glass, looked at it and put it down again. "All this is in confidence," he said. "Isn't it?"

"Of course," I said again.

"Thank you, Sheila. And you'll let me know if anything turns up in her papers?" he asked.

"I don't think there's likely to be any- thing," I said. "Not in the stuff I have. I don't think she was one for putting things down on paper." I thought of the list and how I'd found it. "Nothing specific, anyway." I got up and went over to the desk and picked up the cardboard box. "Well, I'd better be going — I really must sort out these photos. Thank you so much for looking them out."

"Glad to have been of help. Good luck with the Book. I'm sure it will be a splendid thing for the village — just the sort of thing to bring a community together . . ." He was back in his MP mode again and kept up his usual meaningless chat as he showed me out.

I was quite glad to be outside. There had been a sort of intensity about our conversation that had left me tired and glad of the fresh air and the open space around me.

But of course I couldn't walk the length of the village street without meeting somebody. Just as I was passing her cottage, Judith came out.

"Oh, Sheila, lovely to see you. Were you looking for Mary? I think she and Jim have gone to Taunton for the day. She said they might go and look at some stair carpet now the sales are on —"

"No," I said, "it's fine. I've just been to collect these old photos from Toby."

238

"Oh, how exciting. It must be thrilling to go through all those things. You never know what you might find!"

"Well, I don't expect anything special. Just family photos of several generations."

"And you had all those things of Annie's. Was there anything there?"

"Just photos and a few letters — those from her grandfather in the First World War. I think I told you about them. Oh, and a few old newspaper cuttings."

"Newspaper cuttings?"

"About her grandfather, mostly — when he got back from the war."

"Oh, I see. All so interesting. We're all longing to see the Book."

"Well, there's still a bit to do — Mary's been wonderful, so helpful — but it won't appear overnight. There's all the actual publishing stuff to do, so you may have to wait a little while . . ."

I finally managed to reach my car and get away, and all the way home I wondered about Toby and just how important it was for him that Annie kept quiet about Max Holtby.

CHAPTER SEVENTEEN

When I got home I found Annie's list, smoothed it out and looked at it again. Most of the villagers, represented by these initials, I'd already considered. All that remained were the Tuckers and Captain Prosser. I didn't count Phyll because she wasn't in the village when Annie was taken ill. It struck me that one person whose name wasn't on the list was Judith, and yet she'd been most assiduous, indeed enthusiastic, in her support for Annie. It looked as though Annie hadn't needed any special hold over Judith; Judith just wanted to be her friend. I wondered what the late Mr. Lamb had thought of Annie and if the friendship had blossomed only when he died and Judith was lonely and needed someone with whom to continue her endless conversation.

Obviously the person who had most to gain by Annie's death was Toby. It was all very well to say that he was giving up at the next election; while Annie was alive he was very much a sitting MP who'd have had a great deal to lose if she'd given even the slightest hint of what she'd overheard. It takes so little to ruin the reputation of even a minor public figure. And because of that threat Diana was not only destroying herself but was fast becoming a loose cannon. Toby must have been fearful of what she might say when she'd had too much to drink, especially if she'd been the one who'd done the actual deed. I thought about my meetings with Diana since Annie's death. I'd seen her only a couple of times, but it seemed to me that she was noticeably more relaxed and certainly perfectly sober.

I didn't believe that any secret the Tuckers had could have provided a greater motive for Annie's murder than Toby's. Still, just to finish things off neatly, as it were, I thought I might as well go and see Ellen.

"I just called on the off chance," I said, "to give you back these photos. I've kept the ones we're using, of course, but I wanted to return the others."

"You shouldn't have bothered," Ellen said, removing a pile of ironing from a chair so that I could sit down opposite her at the kitchen table. "To tell you the truth, we never look at them from one year's end to the other. You don't, really, unless there's a special occasion."

"Well," I said, "I'm always nervous about looking after other people's photographs, especially these old ones that are irreplaceable."

"Fred's uncle Bert was a great one for taking photos. He'd been given this camera — a box Brownie, I suppose it was — one birthday when he was a lad and he went round the farm taking pictures of everything. They all laughed at him, of course — who'd want to look at pictures of old carts and things? Well, I suppose you don't think at the time, do you?"

"Well, I'm very grateful to Fred's uncle Bert," I said. "And what about the groups? They're wonderful."

"Oh, that was Miss Percy. Fred's grandfather used to tell him all about her — she ran everything. She was the rector's sister. His wife was delicate, as they used to say, and didn't do much in the village. She spent a lot of time abroad at those spas in Germany with her old governess — there was no shortage of money — so Miss Percy took charge. She did a lot for the village; woodcarving lessons for the boys (there's a beautiful lectern in the church that they made) and sewing classes for the girls — she paid for all the wood and the material. And outings for the villagers."

"Oh yes, that wonderful photo of everyone crowded into a wagonette!"

"Fred's grandfather said they went to a church festival at Sampford Brett; a lot of them had never been so far from home before!"

"Amazing, isn't it!"

"Well, you forget, don't you, how comparatively recent everything is."

"I must certainly add a bit about Miss Percy in the book. She left a trust, you know, some money for the village, but it's being wound up now."

I told her what Michael had told me and how Annie had held out against it.

"Good for her!" Ellen said. "Whatever else you might say about her, she did care about the village. I suppose it's because she was born and brought up here. There aren't many of us left now."

"And you don't have any relations left in the village?"

"Not since my parents died. My brother's in Bristol and I've got a cousin who's the keeper on the estate at Barton Regis, but that's it."

"That is sad, isn't it?"

"Well, what do you expect — there's nothing for the young people here and I suppose, whatever I think of them, the off-comers keep the village going."

"Annie certainly had them organized," I said, "though I get the feeling that people didn't really *like* her."

"She wasn't one who cared about being liked," Ellen said with a short laugh. "But she certainly got things done."

"Because she had a hold over some people?" I suggested tentatively.

Ellen looked at me sharply. "What sort of hold?"

"A different one for each person, I believe. Most of us have something, however trivial, that we would prefer the world not to know about."

There was a moment's silence. Then Ellen got up. "I'll put the kettle on — you'll have a cup of tea?"

"That would be nice."

Neither of us spoke while she made the tea and got out a tin and put some small cakes onto a plate.

"Bought cake," she said. "My mother would have had a fit."

I smiled. "We all come to it sooner or later, and you're busier than most."

She poured the tea and I took a small

almond slice.

"You're right, of course," she said. "She did have something on us, Fred and me. It was never out in the open, nothing you could really get hold of, just implied. But that was enough. I never supposed we were the only ones, but, of course, she never said anything. I think we all knew — the whole village — but no one had the nerve to stand up to her."

"One person did," I said.

"Really? That was brave. No, I won't ask you who it was because you wouldn't tell me."

"No."

Ellen put some sugar in her tea and stirred it thoughtfully.

"When you get right down to it, our secret wasn't really so dreadful. Most people would think nothing of it. I suppose it was the way Annie put things, those remarks that made you think that everyone would — well, I don't know — would think less of you, I suppose."

"I can imagine."

"And really these days no one would think anything of it — it was just the boys. Fred didn't want them to feel bad, though they both knew, of course." She looked at me and laughed. "You haven't the faintest idea what I'm talking about!"

I shook my head.

"It's the old story, really. Mark isn't Fred's child. I was pregnant when he married me."

"Look, please," I said, "don't feel you have to tell me anything."

"No, I want to — just to prove to myself what an unimportant thing it was and how *stupid* we were to let Annie get at us like that!"

"It's understandable; she was very insidious."

"That's just about it," Ellen said. "Insidious — a nasty word for a nasty person. Well, what happened was that when I was eighteen I went up to Bristol to look after my auntie May. She was my mother's older sister, never married, stayed at home to look after their parents so they left her the little money they had and she managed on that. Anyway, she had this bad go of pneumonia and my mother sent me up to nurse her. Before I went, Fred and I had come to a sort of understanding — not an engagement; both our parents said we were too young. Fred was only a year older than me. So I think my mother was quite glad of an excuse to get me away from the village for a bit."

She picked up the teapot. "Do you want

another cup?"

I shook my head.

"Auntie May had a very good next door neighbor, you know, popping in and out to see if everything was okay. Mrs. Philips she was, Edna. She was very helpful to me and used to bring in meals for us both to save me cooking. Her son Trevor used to bring them round sometimes (he was on leave from the army) and stayed chatting. Then, when Auntie May was getting better, Mrs. Philips used to say, 'You young people go out and enjoy yourselves — I'll sit with May.' So we went to the cinema, for walks on the Downs, or just for a drink. He was very lively, full of fun — older than me, knew his way around. I thought he was wonderful. Well, one thing led to another, as they say, and a little while after I got back home I realized how stupid I'd been."

"Did you tell Fred?"

"Yes, I told him first of all, even before I told my mother. He was very upset, of course, and I felt terrible because I knew it was him I wanted — Trevor was only a bit of madness. I thought I'd ruined everything."

"So what happened?"

"Well, I had to tell my mother and she and my father were furious — you remember how it was, such a disgrace. But Fred said he still wanted to marry me and we should do it right away. I must say, his father was very good about it (his mother had died when he was quite young) and we had the banns called straightaway and Fred's father let us have the farm cottage."

"What about Trevor — did you ever tell him?"

"No, what would have been the use? He wasn't one for settling down. Anyway, I heard a few years later that he'd been killed on some sort of military exercise. Very sad; he'd been so full of life." She sat quietly for a moment, looking down at her clasped hands. "Still, I suppose in some ways it was for the best; it might have been awkward later on."

"Does Mark look like him?" I asked.

"Not really; just occasionally there's something."

"Perhaps that's why he chose to go into the army."

"Perhaps. He never wanted to do anything on the farm. Just as well, really. I mean, Fred always treated him as his own, but I think he's glad Dan will have the farm — well, it's been in the family for generations; you know how it is . . ."

"How were the boys when you told them?"

"They'd always been very close — Dan looked up to Mark and, of course, by the time they were old enough for us to tell them it wasn't such a big deal; people's attitudes had changed. No, they took it very well. I suppose because Dan was so set on farming and Mark wasn't, that made it easier. No, bless them, they're still very good friends. But Fred was right; it would have been awkward for them if word had got about. That's why we fell in with what Annie wanted."

"How could she have found out?" I asked.

"There was a bit of talk in the village when Fred and I got married so young and then Mark being born so soon after. But I suppose people thought we'd just been careless. But Martha, Annie's mother, liked ferreting out bits of gossip. That's probably where Annie got it from."

"Such a horrible, spiteful thing to do, to hold it over you like that," I said.

"And, as you say, we weren't the only ones. It's an awful thing to say, but there's quite a lot of people in the village who'll feel better now she's gone." She got up and took the teapot over to the sink. "I'm glad I told you, Sheila. In a funny sort of way it puts it into perspective."

"I'm glad you did," I said. "Of course, I'd

never mention it to anyone . . ." I got up and moved towards the door. "I'll see you soon. Take care of yourself."

The next day I had to take Tris to have his nails clipped. Unlike Foss, who loves attention of any kind, Tris hates going to the vet. From the moment we go through the door he starts whining and insists on sitting on my knee shivering pathetically. There appeared to be only one vet on duty and the waiting room was full, so it looked as if we were in for a long wait. However, the door opened and I was pleased to see Rachel coming in with Phyll's old Labrador, who sank down heavily at her feet, snuffling occasionally but otherwise unmoved.

I greeted Rachel and bent over to pat him. "Is he all right?"

"Yes, he's just here for his booster shot. Phyll would have brought him but she and Martin wanted to go to Taunton."

"He's still staying with you?" I asked.

"Oh yes. As a matter of fact I was going to ring you and Rosemary to tell you the news. Phyll and Martin are engaged."

"Good heavens! But they hardly know each other!"

"I know. But actually they more or less fell for each other that time in Madeira. A real *coup de foudre,* from what I can gather, at least on Phyll's part, and I believe he felt much the same. But Martin had an ailing wife and Phyll had decided to devote her life to looking after Father, so they parted forever — or so they thought. She was very upset when they came home; she'd never really been in love before, poor lamb. You can imagine the long phone calls telling me all about it! Anyway, when he turned up again in this totally unexpected way and a widower, it wasn't so much a question of if they'd get together, but when."

"How extraordinary — like something out of a Victorian novel. The sort of coincidence you think only happens in books, though life is full of them! They certainly seem fond of each other — a real happy ending! How do you feel about it?"

"Oh, I'm delighted for Phyll. She adored Father and this is the first time I've seen her really happy since he died."

"And what do you think about Martin?"

She shrugged. "I really don't know. He seems genuinely attached to her, which is the important thing. We don't know much about him but there probably isn't that much to know, if you see what I mean."

"What you see is what you get?"

"I think so."

"I must say I do see what you mean about Phyll being happy. They were telling me about renovating the cottage and she was absolutely bubbling over with excitement, and he was amused but in a fond sort of way."

"Perhaps fond is the word, but it's quite a good sort of love, isn't it, and it isn't as if either of them is in the first flush of youth. I think he will make her happy and that's what matters."

"And how about you? If they move into Annie's cottage — when Phyll's altered it to her satisfaction! — you'll be left alone in that big house."

"Oh, we'll cross that bridge when we come to it. With all the ideas Phyll has about the cottage — not to mention changing her mind about everything half a dozen times — it'll be the best part of a year before they actually move."

"And what about the wedding — when will that be?"

"They haven't decided yet, but fairly soon, I think. There's no reason for them to wait and it's going to be quite a simple affair. They'll speak to Father William about it sometime soon."

"Well," I said, "I think that's simply splendid. Are they telling people, or should

I keep it a secret?"

"Oh no, they want everyone to know. In fact, I said I'd organize an engagement party. I do hope you and Rosemary will come."

"I'd love to, of course," I said, "and I'm sure Rosemary will too."

"What an extraordinary thing," Rosemary said when I told her. "I just hope Phyll knows what she's doing. After all, what do we know about Martin? I mean, it was odd enough the way he turned out to be Annie's cousin and turned up here. She's only known him for a few weeks."

"And that time in Madeira."

"A holiday romance!"

"Dr. Gregory liked him — I'm sure that weighed a lot with Phyll."

"Liking him on holiday's one thing, but Dr. G never expected him to want to marry his daughter."

"I think Michael made some inquiries about him when it turned out he inherited everything from Annie. I'm sure if there'd been anything fishy, he'd have discovered it."

"I suppose so."

"So will you come to the engagement party?"

"Of course! And I really do hope everything will turn out well for them. It's just that I'm fond of old Phyll and I think she's taking a bit of a risk."

"All marriage is a risk in one way or other. I don't see why this shouldn't work out perfectly well."

"You're probably right. Goodness, is that the time? I must go — I've got to take Mother her prescription. Still, at least I'll have a hot piece of news for her. Mulling over this will keep her happy for days!"

CHAPTER EIGHTEEN

Rachel's engagement party for Phyll and Martin was a great success — lots of people, delicious food and an excited buzz. The only drawback was that the guests (given the presence of the two people involved) hesitated to speculate among themselves on the surprising and fascinating nature of the news, though Anthea did manage to back me into a corner and make her views known.

"It's all a bit sudden, isn't it?" she demanded in a rather too-loud voice.

"Well . . . ," I began.

"He's only been in the village five minutes and here's Phyllis Gregory marrying him!"

"Oh, they'd known each other before," I said. "Her father liked him very much."

"What do you mean? Dr. Gregory? He's been dead for years."

"They knew him in Madeira ages ago," I said. "Didn't you know?" I added provocatively. "Long before either of them knew he was related to Annie. Phyll's been telling everyone about the amazing coincidence."

"Coincidence!" Anthea said disapprovingly. She turned and looked at the happy couple.

"He's not very tall; she'll have to stop wearing high heels. I always think it looks very odd in a couple if a woman is taller than a man. So, when are they getting married? Or is it going to be one of those long engagements?"

"Oh, quite soon, I think — before Christmas, anyway."

"What's the rush?" she asked, obviously disappointed that the bride's age made the possibility of a shotgun wedding unlikely.

"There doesn't seem any reason to wait and it's going to be a simple ceremony, so there won't be a lot of preparations to make."

"Well, I must say I think it's very hard on Rachel, coming all the way down here from Scotland to be with her sister and then having her go off like this."

"They'll still be in the village," I said. "They're having Annie's cottage done up — Phyll is full of it!"

"I wouldn't care to live right in the village like that, and it's a dismal sort of place. No," she said dismissively, "I wouldn't care for that at all."

However, Anthea's seemed to be the lone disapproving voice.

"Splendid news," Captain Prosser said, embarking on his third vol-au-vent. "Couldn't happen to a nicer couple."

"Such an amazing coincidence," Mary Fletcher said. "Meeting again after all those years — quite romantic!"

"And having the cottage," Jim put in, "they've got a ready-made home. Though there must be a lot to do to it."

"I believe it needs complete modernizing," I said.

"Well, Annie never spent a penny on it," Jim said. "Allowed it to get into a very bad state." It was interesting to see how criticism of Annie was now deemed to be allowable. "It's going to cost a packet." He looked around to see if he could be overheard by the happy couple. "I don't know how well-off Martin is; though, of course, he'll be selling his house — or is it a flat — in London and, even these days, London prices are pretty high."

"And I imagine," Captain Prosser said, lowering his voice, "there's no shortage of money on *her* side."

"I believe Dr. Gregory had private means,"

Jim said confidentially, "and so did his wife."

They all looked at me as someone who had known the family for years.

"They always seemed comfortably off," I said vaguely. I started to move away. "Do excuse me; I must have a word with Father William."

He was standing at the far end of the room by the table with the food. "Now," he said earnestly, "shall I have just one more of these delicious anchovy tartlets, or shall I go straight on to that irresistible chocolate cake?"

"Decisions, decisions!" I said, smiling. "Go for the cake, and then you could fit in a piece of the cherry cheesecake, which is Rachel's specialty, as well."

"Of course! Local knowledge, always so useful."

"So what do you think?" I asked. "Is it going to work?"

"I don't see why not. They are both of mature years and seem well suited."

"I suppose so. It's just that we don't know much about him."

"What do we really know about anyone?" He looked at me quizzically. "No doubt he has secrets like the rest of us. If Phyllis is prepared to take him on trust, perhaps we should too."

"Possibly," I said doubtfully, "but she's . . . well, prejudiced in his favor."

"The eye of love? You may be right, but that may not always be a bad thing. That particular gaze may very well penetrate into places where the casual glance cannot reach. Don't you agree?"

I laughed. "Metaphysics, even spurious ones, can win any argument. Anyway, when's the wedding to be? Have they set an actual date?"

"I have to rearrange a few things, but before Christmas, certainly. I gather Phyllis has always wanted to spend Christmas in Vienna, so that is where they will spend their honeymoon."

"Dear Phyll," I said affectionately, "a genuine romantic!"

"That is, naturally, top secret information and I've only told you now because I know that your implacable curiosity would have wheedled it out of me sooner or later."

"Of course, not a word! And I'll feign total surprise when I'm finally told."

I looked round the room. "Is it my imagination or is the atmosphere quite different now than it was at other gatherings — the Harvest Supper, for example — when Annie was alive? Everyone seems much more relaxed."

"I think we both know the answer to that." He cut a thick slice of chocolate cake and placed it carefully on a plate. "Have you made any progress? In general terms, that is."

"In general terms. I've found, as we agreed, that everyone has some sort of secret they would prefer to keep hidden. Mostly minor ones, though there are a couple that might cause more anxiety. I really don't know. It was such a calculated thing to do." I paused. "As I say, I don't know."

"Come and see me sometime if you think it would help. Come anyway and have a glass of delicious sherry . . ." He picked up a fork and began to eat. "Absolutely *divine*. I can't imagine how you could resist it."

Like Max Beerbohm, I love the seaside out of season when the visitors and day-trippers have gone, the amusement arcades are shuttered, the cheap clothing shops are closed and the beach is empty except for the occasional dog walker. Then the town reverts to its old self, what it was like in my parents' time. I like it best when there is a brisk wind and there are curling white horses on the sea and the clouds part to let through an occasional gleam of sunshine. The next day was just such a day, so I called Tris, held him still while I fastened his coat (he's quite an elderly dog now and feels the cold), and got down his lead. Foss, who'd investigated the weather earlier in the day and rejected it, gave us a contemptuous look and took himself upstairs to sleep under the duvet.

I didn't go down to the harbor, but farther along the seafront, to where the receding tide had left the sort of firm sand that suits Tris's short legs. I let him off the lead and he ran away, barking at seagulls and investigating the clumps of seaweed, as if the briskness of the day had somehow renewed his youth. I followed more slowly, pausing to look for shells and bits of driftwood, but beachcombing here usually offers nothing more than empty plastic bottles and other, even less agreeable detritus. As I walked, thinking of William's offer, I tried to sort out in my mind what exactly I had discovered, trying to fit together some sort of coherent picture from the diverse pieces of information I'd gleaned.

As I'd told William, most of the secrets were of a fairly minor nature. Their revelation might have caused a certain embarrassment to the people involved, but there was nothing that wouldn't have been a nine days' wonder in the village. Ellen's boys might (or might not) have felt uncomfortable if the truth had come out, but — as we'd agreed — in this day and age there was no reason why they should. And, actually, I had no way of knowing if my theory about the Fletchers' son was true and I had only a vague feeling about the Sanderses' daughter. Nor did I know if Maurice was in the pay of the developers and had wanted to displace Annie on the committee of the village trust.

The only two people I really did know about who might have been harmed by Annie's threats were Naomi and Toby. Well, Naomi couldn't be actually harmed, because the medical scandal she was involved in would surely be known to her present employers. But it would be a real blow to her pride to have it all dragged out into the open.

Which left Toby. Thinking back to our conversation I realized I'd been rather carried away by the feeling of nostalgia from the photos. Toby admitted that there had been dealings with Max Holtby, and, even if there'd been nothing actually illegal, Annie knew enough to make things very difficult for him. He certainly had the most to lose and that, of course, explained his particular dislike of Annie and his unease in her presence. It must have been like living with a time bomb. And Diana must have been involved. She really hated Annie and, in spite of the danger to Toby, let it show. Toby was weak, but, somehow, I felt that Diana might well have had the resolution to get rid of Annie. Certainly she'd been quite different since Annie had died.

A loud barking made me look for Tris and I saw he was confronting a young golden retriever. As I went towards him a familiar voice behind me called out, "Flora, come here. Come here at once!" I turned round and saw that it was Diana.

"It's all right, Sheila. She's quite harmless — only wants to play."

Tris, having recovered from his surprise, decided that he too would like to play and they raced up and down the beach together, scattering sand in all directions.

"Sorry about that," Diana said. "She's a bit excitable."

We both looked at Flora, who, having totally ignored Diana's command, at that moment decided to splash about in a rock pool, and emerged dripping. I laughed, then said, "Dogs! But it would be awful to be without one."

"When Tessa, my old retriever, died, I was so upset that I made a vow I'd never have another one. That lasted a week."

"I know."

We stood for a moment watching the dogs. I'd never seen Diana in this mood before. It was almost as if the stiff breeze had blown away her usual supercilious manner.

"Toby told me about your visit," Diana said.

"Oh yes, the photos."

"Not just the photos. About that bloody woman."

"She had some sort of hold over a lot of people," I said, "if that's any sort of consolation."

"But not like the one she had over Toby. She could have ruined him."

"Well, yes, I suppose so."

"And didn't she just love that!" Diana said viciously. "Her mother used to do the washing for his family when times were hard before the war. So she really enjoyed having that sort of power over him. People in the village have long memories."

"Especially for slights, real or fancied."

"She liked to play games — you know, hints, double meanings, never quite saying anything, just keeping us on edge all the time."

I remembered her jibes to him about

politicians' memoirs. "I bet she did," I said.

"When we were first married and I came here to live, she was all over us; nothing was too much trouble. And when I was laid up with a bad leg that had to have the dressings changed every day, she was in and out the whole time. But, of course, we didn't know then . . ."

"That was how she gathered her information?" I said.

"It was worse for me, of course, because I was down here most of the time — I'm useless at constituency things, though I did my best — so I was the main target. She really enjoyed that."

I could just imagine Annie's delight in taking Diana down a peg. "Yes," I said, "she'd like that."

Diana was silent for a moment, apparently concentrating on taking deep breaths of sea air.

Then she said, "I'm so glad she's dead."

"A horrible way to die."

"It was typical — she always had to know best. Well, that time she didn't and it killed her." Her voice was hard. "In fact," she went on, "if she hadn't died when she did, I do believe I would have killed her myself."

"You don't mean that," I said.

She'd been staring out to sea, but now

she turned and looked at me. "What? I don't know — perhaps, if she'd gone on . . ."

"Toby said he's giving up at the next general election."

"He's been living on the edge for too long. I hated to see him like that. It was never really his thing, you know; he was pushed into it. I'd have done anything . . . Still, it's all right now."

The dogs came rushing up; Tris was panting a little and I bent down and put his lead back on. The retriever shook herself briskly, covering us both with sandy water. Diana grabbed her collar.

"Sorry, Sheila," she said, her words seeming to cover both the wetting and our conversation.

"That's fine," I said. "I think I'd better get this one home — he's not used to such energetic exercise."

She bent and patted Tris. "He's a splendid little chap." Flora, meanwhile, had wrenched herself free and was racing off towards the sea. "I'd better go after her," she said, "before she tries to swim to Wales! Anyway, I can do with a good walk; it clears the head somehow." She gave me one of her rare smiles and set off along the beach.

As I was trying to get most of the sand off Tris's paws before I put him in the car, I looked up and saw that she was racing along, the dog leaping beside her, like a young girl — like her mythical namesake.

"It was a really odd feeling," I said to Rosemary when I saw her next day, "seeing her like that — natural and not being sarcastic all the time or scoring points."

"Doesn't sound like the Diana we know."

"Though she was really bitter and savage about Annie. I did think —"

"That she might have poisoned her?"

"It would have been easy for her to go across the field (her field) and get in the back way."

"You think she's bright enough to have planned something like that?"

"Oh, Diana's bright enough. But . . . well . . . I'm not so sure now."

"You don't think she could have killed anyone because she loves dogs?" Rosemary looked at me quizzically.

"And horses too." I laughed. "No, there was something about the way she talked about wanting to kill her."

"That could have been to put you off the scent."

"It could. As I said, she's bright enough. No, it was just the way she spoke. Oh, I don't know. Toby certainly had enough motive to want Annie out of the way and, since he wasn't around when she died, then it would have to be Diana . . ."

Rosemary looked at me with a slight smile. "Has it ever occurred to you that no one killed Annie Roberts, that it really was an accident?"

"You mean that I'm making a mystery out of nothing?"

"Something like that."

"But all those people — they all loathed her."

"Just because a lot of people loathed her, it doesn't mean that someone killed her."

"But we know for a fact that she found out their secrets and used them to manipulate people."

"But you have no proof that anybody actually got rid of her."

"Well, no . . ."

"Exactly. So let it be."

"You're right," I said reluctantly. "As usual. I'm making too much of things."

"Well, put it out of your mind and come into Taunton with me to find Mother a new bedspread. There's nothing in Taviscombe and she won't consider catalogues, even the really fancy ones, and when we offered to order her one online she nearly had a fit!"

"Does she really need a new bedspread?"
I asked.

Rosemary gave a short, mirthless laugh.
"When has *need* ever entered into it! No,
she said that she got sick and tired of looking at it when she was in bed ill. I know
perfectly well, before I even set out, that
whatever I bring will have to go back again.
It's going to be a difficult task, so be
prepared to bend your mind to it. *But,* while
we're there we could reward ourselves with
lunch at that rather glamorous new place in
the precinct."

CHAPTER NINETEEN

When I woke up a few days later I felt somehow a lightening of spirits, and then I remembered that I'd agreed with Rosemary to abandon all thoughts of foul play where Annie's death was concerned. Energized by this feeling, I embarked on the distasteful task of defrosting the ancient freezer in the larder. It was wedged up in the corner and soon I was uncomfortably surrounded by trays of frozen packages, most of which I discovered with shame were well past their use-by dates. The defrosting took ages, even with the help of my hair dryer, and, when I'd finally got the usable things back in again, my back was aching and my hands were frozen.

I'd just put the kettle on for a much-needed cup of tea when the telephone rang; it was Mary Fletcher with a query about the Book.

"Sorry to bother you," she said, "but I

thought I ought to make sure it was all right before it goes off to the printer."

I assured her (mendaciously) that it was no bother and that I'd ring her back as soon as I'd checked. Then I fed the animals again to placate them for having been banished from the kitchen when I was busy, and resolutely sat down to rest my back with a cup of tea and a slice of coffee sponge before I got out the folders. I found the thing Mary had queried quite quickly, but as I picked up the folders to put them back in my desk, I dropped one and the contents scattered everywhere. As I replaced them I noticed a few old newspaper cuttings that had been caught up behind the minutes of a parish council meeting that I hadn't bothered to look at before. I was turning them over casually when I came to one that stopped me in my tracks.

It was dated some years before and had been cut out from one of the more sensational Sunday tabloids. The headline read "Where Are They Now?" and below it said "Was this really Justice? These were piffling little sentences on men who ruined the lives of innocent people. Now they're free to get on with their own lives, unlike their poor victims who still suffer."

There were three columns, each devoted

to some criminal: a hit-and-run driver, a businessman who set up a Christmas Club scam, and a solicitor. The headline for the last one read "Midland Solicitor Jailed for Fraud" and the photograph below it bore the caption "Donald Lee entering the court with his wife, Jennifer." Below this was the original news item. Donald Lee had been the senior partner in a thriving practice with branches throughout the Midlands, but he had been systematically taking money from his clients' accounts. They were all elderly people, usually with no near relatives to look out for them. The judge said in his summing-up that this was a particularly despicable crime since it betrayed the trust of some of the most vulnerable members of society. He was sentenced to three years. The woman in the photo was unmistakably Judith.

I sat for a while, not quite able to take in what I'd just read; then I detached the cutting and put everything else away. Dutifully I phoned Mary and answered her query. Then I phoned Rosemary.

"Are you busy? Can I come round?"

"Yes, do come. I was just making a sandwich for lunch — come and join me. What is it? Has something happened?"

"In a way, but nothing awful. I'll come

right away."

Rosemary opened the door to me with a question on her lips; then, thinking better of it, she followed me into the kitchen and waited until I'd sat down.

"Now, then," she said, "whatever is it?"

I took the cutting from my bag and laid it on the table. Rosemary picked it up and read it, put it down and then picked it up and read it again.

"Well!" she said. "Fancy that!"

"I know," I said. "It knocked me sideways too."

She got up and went over to the kettle. "No," she said, "tea is quite inadequate. What we need is a drink."

She poured two large glasses of wine and put a plate of sandwiches on the table between us.

"Now, then. What an extraordinary thing."

"It was caught up behind some boring council meeting papers that I never bothered to read. I found it quite by accident. We might never have known; I was going to give the papers back to Martin next week."

"Poor Judith. It must have been awful for her. All the time he was in prison — and I bet people were horrible to her — then having to change their name and coming down here and trying to make a new life."

"And then Annie finds out," I said, "and uses it . . ."

"To make a slave of her."

"Yes."

"Did Judith ever talk about her husband?"

"Desmond? I think she called him Desmond. No, come to think of it, considering how much she *did* talk, she hardly ever mentioned him. I gather he died quite soon after they came to the village."

"So he was probably dead when Annie came across that thing in the newspaper?"

I picked up the cutting and checked the date. "He must have done."

"So she never blackmailed him, only Judith."

"From the sound of it, I don't think he was the sort of man you would blackmail. Too devious for an amateur like Annie."

"So it was only poor little Judith."

"It looks like it. Mind you," I said, "that's assuming Judith hasn't been putting on an act all these years. For all we know, she might have known what was going on — might even have been part of it."

We looked at each other. "No way," Rosemary said. "No one could keep up that sort of woolly-mindedness so long!"

"You're right; you'd have to be a consummate actress to carry that off, and Judith certainly isn't that!" I took a sandwich. "Delicious ham — where did you get it?"

"The farm shop. Their stuff's really good."

After a moment I said, "What's so extraordinary is the way she was with Annie. I mean, she acted as if Annie really was her friend."

"Mm. I think that after a while she persuaded herself to believe it. It was probably easier than facing up to how Annie actually controlled her."

"Yes, I think you're right. I imagine Judith always took the easiest way out. I expect that's how she coped with what her husband did."

"I wonder what he was like? The husband, I mean. People in the village don't seem to mention him. Perhaps he was the sort of man who stayed in the background. He'd certainly have a good reason to."

I picked up the cutting again. "He looks quite innocuous in the photo." I said.

"So did Crippen!"

I laughed. "But he wasn't a murderer." I stopped. "But what about Judith?"

"Oh dear, I thought we'd decided there wasn't a murder. And Judith — I can't believe it!"

"But think," I said. "This is almost the

strongest motive we've had yet!"

"Oh, come on!"

"Just think what a particularly beastly crime it was — stealing from all those poor old souls! Judith would never have been able to hold her head up again in the village, and being part of the village was her whole life, after he'd gone."

"I suppose . . ."

"And it would have been so easy for her; she was in and out of Annie's house the whole time, knew exactly what she was doing practically every minute of the day, so she knew when Annie would be out and for how long, so that she could substitute the poisonous fungi for the safe ones."

"But she wouldn't have known about them."

"She might have done. I bet Annie went on about her expertise all the time."

Rosemary sighed. "Well, I suppose it's possible. But, oh dear, I did think we'd drawn a line under the whole thing."

"But then," I said, "we didn't know about this." I picked up the cutting and looked at it again.

"It's so extraordinary to have found it like that, just when I was going to give all the stuff back to Martin. It seems almost as if it's meant —"

"Now, Sheila," Rosemary said severely, "don't make it an excuse to start that business all over again."

I put the cutting down and took another sandwich. "You're probably right," I said, "but I can't help wondering. Did you see, they kept their proper initials — Donald Lee to Desmond Lamb and Jennifer Lee to Judith Lamb. I suppose it made things easier. I wonder what people in the village —"

"Sheila!"

"Oh, all right."

"So Desmond, Donald, whatever you like to call him, was a crook and Judith — she doesn't *look* like a Jennifer, does she? — was being blackmailed by Annie. So what? Why would she suddenly want to kill Annie after all that time. He died years ago and Judith quite liked the idea of being Annie's best friend."

"Well . . . yes, I do see what you mean," I said doubtfully. "But there may have been some sort of quarrel and Annie could have threatened to reveal all!"

"Unlikely. A quarrel would mean Judith standing up to Annie and that's something she'd never do."

"True."

"Right, then, that's settled. Oh yes, I've

been longing to tell you — Mother actually *liked* that bedspread we found."

"No!"

"Of course, I told her that *you* chose it. 'Sheila has very good taste,' she said!"

We both giggled like schoolgirls.

When I got home I carefully replaced the newspaper cutting behind the council minutes, where I'd found it. Somehow I didn't want anyone else, carelessly flicking through the papers, to see it. I felt that this thing I'd found out about Judith should remain hidden, as it had been for so many years. I was about to close the folder when I came across an envelope. It was addressed to Annie, but there was nothing in it. Idly I turned it over and there, on the back in Annie's writing, I saw "*Captain* Prosser? I don't think so. Chief Petty Officer — if that!"

Suddenly a great wave of dislike for Annie swept over me. Even this poor, sad little secret hadn't been hidden from Annie and she'd made use of it.

On an impulse I bundled up all the folders and put them in a carrier bag. Next day I'd take them back to Martin. Once they were out of the house there'd be no temptation to go rummaging about on the off chance of finding anything else. I felt I'd already found out quite enough.

Martin was out but Phyll invited me in.

"Martin's had to go up to London," she said excitedly. "He's had an offer for his flat. Isn't that marvellous? We thought it would be so difficult to sell, things being as they are. But one of his colleagues has to move down to London from Manchester and he thinks it might be just what he wants. Isn't that lucky! I mean, we could have been waiting for ages to get it sorted."

"That's splendid," I said. "So how are the wedding plans going? Have you got your dress yet?"

"It was a bit difficult. As you can imagine, at my age I didn't want anything long and white with a veil — all that — but I do want something special."

"Of course you do."

"Well, Rachel drove me over to Bath, to a little boutique there. I'd never heard of it, of course, and it's fearfully expensive. But, oh, Sheila, they had some beautiful things!"

"So what did you choose?"

"Hang on and I'll show you!" She jumped up and rushed out of the room, just as Rachel came in.

"Hello," she said. "I thought I heard voices."

"I came to leave some stuff for Martin, but Phyll's gone to get her wedding dress for me to see."

Rachel smiled. "She's very excited."

"She looks sixteen again," I said. "Just like she was when Miss Brabourne made her captain of hockey — do you remember?"

"Do I not! But, really, it's lovely to see her so happy."

Phyll came back bearing a dress on a hanger. "There! Isn't it gorgeous?"

"Oh, it's beautiful," I said. And it was. A silk dress in a soft shade of blue with a draped bodice. "Hold it up against you so that I can see."

"We thought a long skirt," Rachel said, "but not full length."

"Oh, Rache chose it," Phyll said.

"It's perfect," I said, "and that blue brings out the color of your eyes. I'm glad to see that it's got long sleeves. The church is very cold, especially at this time of the year."

"Father William said he'll leave the heat on all night the night before," Rachel said, "so that should help. Anyway, Sheila, now that you're here, stay and have a cup of coffee and" — smiling affectionately at Phyll — "*she* will tell you all about the arrangements for the reception."

■ ■ ■ ■

As I drove home I thought how good it was to see them together again. Phyll had seemed to drift along after her father died, not exactly unhappy, but aimless, as if she'd lost her sense of direction. But now that her strong, loving elder sister had come back, she'd become a different person. Much more her old self, more relaxed and happy, even before Martin had reappeared in her life. But (and the thought startled me so much that I felt obliged to pull into a lay-by to consider it) was it just that, or was it because Annie was dead? Somehow I'd forgotten that her initials were on Annie's list. Well, not forgotten exactly, but it was a thought I'd put to one side because, since she was away from the village when Annie was taken ill, I hadn't considered her as a suspect. But if she was on that list, she must have had a secret. I started the car again and resolutely put it out of my mind. So what if she did have a secret? It wasn't important and I really didn't want to know.

As I was getting breakfast the next morning I switched on the radio and heard a familiar voice:

281

". . . We are told that you should love your neighbor. More than that — it's quite specific — you must love your neighbor as yourself. A hard thing to ask. Not all neighbors are lovable; some may be unpleasant, even wicked. Must we love them? And then, we may ask, who *is* my neighbor? The preacher John Donne — who was also a poet and saw things with the clear eye of a poet — provides one answer. 'No man is an island,' he says. 'I am involved in Mankind.' We are all connected to one another as human beings and I would ask you, today, to look at each person you meet in your daily life — whatever your opinion of them may be — with a fresh eye, as first of all a fellow human being. Part, like you, of mankind."

Here was a moment's silence, then the announcer's voice. "Thought for the Day was given by Father William Faber."

I switched off the radio and considered what William had said. I thought of the other words of Donne's sermon. "Any man's death diminishes me . . . And therefore never send to know for whom the bell tolls: It tolls for thee." When words are so familiar the mind slides over them without examining them properly. Everyone in the village (a microcosm, you might say, of Mankind) was involved with Annie. She was hardly a good neighbor, but her death affected them all. But it *was* hard to think of Annie first of all as a human being. A hard thing to ask, William had said — I wasn't sure I could do that. But then I thought of the picture of Annie, a little girl in a summer frock, standing up close to her mother on a sunny day many years ago.

Life does things to people. We should, I suppose, try to understand. It was all very complicated; perhaps I would talk to William about it one day.

A sharp bark at the back door and a reproachful feline face at the window reminded me to let the animals in, feed them, make my breakfast and generally get on with my life.

CHAPTER TWENTY

The wedding went off very well. "All brides are supposed to look radiant," I whispered to Rosemary as Phyll came down the aisle, "but she really does." The reception was in the village hall, though there were outside caterers. "Rache wanted to do it," Phyll had told me, "but I said she must just enjoy herself without all the fuss and responsibility!" I looked around the hall. Most of the village seemed to be there — after all, it really was a most unexpected match and decidedly an Event. I caught William's eye and he smiled and raised his glass. "Really good champagne," Captain Prosser had said approvingly, "not any old stuff."

Diana came over to speak to me. "Quite an occasion," she said. "Fancy old Phyll getting off at last." A typical Diana remark, but she sounded amused and almost affectionate, unlike her usual sarcastic self.

"I know," I said. "Isn't it splendid? She's

so happy."

"What about him? Is he okay?"

"He seems nice, and fond of Phyll. Anyway, Rachel likes him and she's nobody's fool, so I think he's all right."

"Yes, Rachel — it must be a bit hard on her, when she's just moved back here, to be left rattling about in that big house alone."

"Well, it won't be for a while. Phyll and Martin will stay with her when they get back from their honeymoon, until the cottage is renovated, and that's bound to take ages. And, of course, they'll still be in the village."

"That's true. Toby wanted to come down for the wedding, but there's some tiresome committee he had to be at the House for. I can't wait for him to come back for good. I hate London and all that political nonsense. *He* was never cut out for it — pretty well forced into it by our families." She smiled. "He can be himself at last, the man I thought I'd married."

"I'm very happy for you," I said, and I meant it. The new Diana seemed to be an agreeable person and I was glad to wish her well.

"Thanks. I think they're about to cut the cake and have the toasts, so I'd better get a refill." She held up her glass, which I noticed had contained orange juice, gave me the ghost of her old sardonic smile and moved toward the buffet.

"Whatever's happened to Diana?" Rosemary had come up behind me. "Is she on the wagon?"

"I think so."

"And she's actually *amiable.* I couldn't believe my ears when I heard her congratulating Phyll as if she really meant it. A complete personality change!"

"I know. I think it's relief. She had to be hard and confrontational because she was unhappy and, probably, afraid."

"Because of Annie, you mean?"

"I think that was the last straw — all that stuff I told you — worrying about it. I'm sure that's why she took to drink. And now that Annie's gone and Toby's retiring, she can relax at last."

"You may be right. Well, whatever it is, it's a vast improvement."

The speeches were short and affectionate — Phyll was very popular in the village — and soon afterwards the happy couple went away.

"So sensible," Mary Fletcher said to me, "not to have to change. I mean, that lovely dress was perfectly all right to travel in. Anyway, they're only going to London today. Rachel said they're staying at the Ritz tonight before they catch their flight to Vienna. Isn't that glamorous!"

"Lovely," I said. "I've always wanted to stay at the Ritz, but I don't suppose I ever will now."

"Oh, you never know your luck! Oh yes, before I forget, the printer said they hope to have finished copies of the book in a few weeks' time, so we must make proper arrangements for distributing them."

"Yes, of course, we'll have a chat about it. Father William has some good ideas. I'll see when he's free and we can all get together."

I had a quick word with Rachel. "It all went off splendidly; you must be very pleased."

"Yes, thank goodness. Phyll had a fit of nerves this morning."

"Not doubts?"

"Oh no — no problem there. She suddenly got panicky at the thought of everyone *looking* at her! Well, you know she's never liked being the center of attention. Anyway, I told her the only person looking at her that mattered was Martin, and that did the trick."

"She certainly looked blissfully happy."

"Yes, I do believe she is. Such a relief."

■ ■ ■ ■

William agreed a time to discuss the arrangements for the Book and Mary was keen for us to meet at her house. Jim was nowhere to be seen and I suspected that he'd been told to make himself scarce. I was touched to see that she'd got out the best china and that there was homemade shortbread and fancy almond biscuits.

"Now, do make yourselves at home. Sheila, you sit here. Father, I think you'll find that chair comfortable. I'll just get the coffee."

After a lot of offers of milk and sugar ("I've got sweeteners somewhere if you'd rather") we finally got down to business, which we settled fairly quickly and efficiently, after which, as is the custom at such times, we relaxed into a good old gossip.

"Such a lovely wedding," Mary said. "A beautiful service, suitable for one of riper years — or is that baptism?"

"I did, certainly, edit it slightly," William said. "I felt they were rather past the age for the procreation of children."

"And so many people there," Mary said hastily. "The village hall was quite crowded.

Judith was saying it was just the sort of thing that Annie would have loved."

There was an almost imperceptible silence; then I said, "Yes, I'm sure she would. Well, I suppose in a way Martin was there because of her — I mean," I continued, feeling that I was not improving matters, "we might never have known him if . . . Though, of course, he and Phyll had met before, so I suppose they *might* have come together again in the general course of things."

"Indeed they might," William said, obviously enjoying my confusion. "God moves in a mysterious way, as the hymn tells us."

"I love Cowper," I said. "So, of course, did Jane Austen — you remember that bit in *Sense and Sensibility*?"

"Some of his poems are really lovely," Mary said, delighted at the literary turn the conversation had taken. "That one about the stricken deer. I often think of that when they're hunting."

At that the conversation proceeded along familiar lines and the old arguments, Mary, a keen supporter of the RSPCA and William mischievously citing the many hunting parsons, which fortunately got us to Jack Russell terriers.

"Well," I said, "do forgive me, but I really must go. I want to drop in on Rachel and return a book."

William got to his feet. "Oh, don't go, Father," Mary said. "There's several things I'd like to ask you about." Obviously, she was determined to make the most of a social occasion.

Rachel looked a little disconcerted when she answered the door.

"Oh, I'm sorry," I said apologetically. "Is this a bad time? I only wanted to return this book that Phyll lent me."

"No, no, it's fine, do come in. It's just that I have to make a rather important phone call and it might take a little while. But come into the sitting room and make yourself at home and then, when I've made the call, we'll have lunch."

"Are you sure?"

"No, really, it'll be nice to have a chat. I'll be as quick as I can." She went out, shutting the door behind her.

I put the book I was returning — *Pruning Shrubs and Roses* — down on the table and went over to the bookshelves, which covered most of one wall. I'm always fascinated by other people's books. Not just what books they have but how they've arranged them, whether orderly (alphabetically, or by subject) or higgledy-piggledy like mine. The books here were quite a mixture. There were a great many Oxford editions of our great authors, presumably from Phyll's school-teaching days, a lot of modern authors in bright dust jackets, and a few medical books left over from Dr. Gregory's time. There was also a fine, handsomely bound collection of the novels of Sir Walter Scott.

I suddenly remembered how, once, when I'd come to tea with Phyll and Rachel when we were quite young, Dr. Gregory read aloud to us from *Ivanhoe,* and how we were all captivated by it. I remembered that the very next day I went to the library to get a copy so I could see how it all turned out. I suppose there are certain authors, certain books even, that you should read when you're young, since it's somehow too daunting to start on them when you're grown up. I went to take down the copy from the shelf, but it wouldn't come out; something seemed to be wedged behind it. By removing *Rob Roy* and *The Heart of Midlothian* from farther along, I was able to get at the book that had been causing the trouble. It was a book on mushrooms and edible fungi. Sticking out from the pages was a slip of paper, marking the place of something. I opened the book and found an entry about the deadly *Lepiota* and its resemblance to the harmless

Macrolepiota. I stared at this for a while; then I saw that the corner of another page had been turned down. This featured a fungus called Brown Roll-Rim, which can be eaten once with no ill effects but, eaten several times, it can cause collapse and possible renal failure. The full implication of what I was looking at suddenly struck me and I was standing there with the book open when Rachel came back into the room.

"Sorry to be so long, but it was something important that I had to arrange —" She saw the book I had in my hand and stopped abruptly.

"I was looking for your father's copy of *Ivanhoe,*" I said.

"Yes."

"And this was wedged behind it."

"I see." She came over and took the book out of my hand, glancing at the page it was open at. "I see," she repeated.

"Rachel," I said urgently, "was it Phyll? I know Annie was blackmailing her — she was blackmailing half the village . . ."

Rachel shook her head slowly. "No. It wasn't Phyll. It was me."

There was complete silence for a moment; then I said, "You did it for Phyll?"

She nodded. "For me as well, in a way." She paused as if to collect her thoughts.

"Annie had been in and out of the house during our mother's last illness and knew that Father had killed our mother." She paused again briefly and went on. "Well, that was how she put it, and I suppose that's how the law would look at it. Because he couldn't bear to see Mother suffer — she was in a great deal of pain — he eased her out of life." Another pause. "That was the hold Annie had."

"But not over your father."

"No, it was a little while after he died. About the time she worked out how to use the knowledge she had of other people's secrets to get power over them — to help her run the village the way she wanted, I suppose. Anyway, you know how devoted Phyll was to Father — she couldn't bear the thought of what people would say."

"People would understand."

"The way she saw it, his good name would be gone, and the respect everyone had for him. She'd been brooding about it for ages and when I came back here she told me all about it."

"Poor Phyll."

"She's my little sister — I had to do something. Besides, I felt the same about Father. I wasn't going to let someone like Annie Roberts destroy his reputation, especially when I thought what a wonderful doctor he'd been and how he'd helped so many people."

I nodded and she went on.

"I knew about her thing with edible fungi so I got this book and found out how the poisonous variety could be mistaken for the harmless one. And then I found the one that you could eat once safely, but was poisonous thereafter. The other two weren't difficult to get hold of, but that one certainly was. I had to go traipsing all over Dorset before I found it. Believe me, I'm quite an expert now. So there you are. I'd found the perfect way to get rid of someone and be nowhere near when it happened."

"But how?" I asked.

"I made several mushroom quiches for the Harvest Supper — one had the Brown Roll-Rim fungus in. I remembered Annie's unpleasant habit of scrounging any leftover food on these occasions and also the fact that she ate up everything, however ancient, in her fridge. I even ate one slice of the quiche myself, and made sure someone saw me, so that, in the unlikely event of anyone questioning what she'd eaten, I could say the quiche was fine. Then I put it to one side as one of the leftovers. And I arranged for Phyll and me to be a long way away when it happened."

"But surely," I said, caught up in her explanation, "you couldn't be sure it would be fatal — not all poisonous fungi actually kill people. She might just have been very ill and then recovered."

"The thing about this particular fungus is that it causes renal failure. I happened to know that Annie had only one kidney. I heard Father mention it — I can't remember the context, but I did remember that. So even a relatively small amount of the stuff, if she ate the whole quiche, would be enough."

"But what about the ones in the house? How did you get them in there?"

"When we came back and heard the news, I helped Judith clear up the house, if you remember. It was easy to leave the back door on the catch — Judith was so busy talking she wouldn't have noticed if I'd left the door wide-open — so I slipped round the back way through the field after dark, and put the poisonous ones in a basket in the kitchen."

We'd been standing all this while, but now she sat down and I felt the need to as well.

After a bit I said, "Does Phyll know?"

"Good God, no! And, please, Sheila, I would be very grateful if you never told her."

"But — but you can't expect me to condone what you've done! I agree that Annie was a despicable person and she made a lot of people thoroughly miserable and she should have been punished. Punished, perhaps, but not *killed*."

"I agree with you. But there was no way of exposing her without the facts coming out. And, from what I gathered, many other facts too, that might have blighted other people's lives."

"You can't justify —"

"No, of course I can't — it's indefensible. All I can do is try and make up for what I've done in other ways."

"What do you mean?"

"The phone call I just made — it was to Jamie's boss at the relief organization. I'm going out to Somalia to one of the refugee camps. They're desperately short of people with medical training."

"It'll be terribly dangerous."

"It's something I can do to make amends, something worthwhile." She gave a wry smile. "I believe it's called expiation. So, please, Sheila, let Annie's death still be an accident — don't tell anyone."

I was silent for a moment. Then I said, "I'll tell Rosemary — she's been puzzled about the whole affair as I have, but she won't tell anyone."

"Thank you. I'm very grateful." She smiled. "Though, actually, I don't think there's any actual evidence . . ."

"There's the book," I said. "Why did you keep it?"

Rachel leaned forwards slightly, as though imparting something secret. "You must *never* think that I'm not aware of what a terrible thing I did; it's burned on my mind. But, just to remind me, every day, I'm taking that book with me — a sort of hair shirt, you might say."

"When are you going?"

"That's what I've just been arranging. I'm going next week."

"But Phyll will still be away on her honeymoon."

"I know. She'd want me to change my mind, ask questions, all sorts of complications. Better to make a clean break. I'll write to her from Cairo. Isn't it wonderfully providential that she has Martin? I worried before about her being lonely again. Now they can live here; I was never very happy about them living in Annie's cottage."

"What about the people in the village? What will you tell them?"

"Oh, anything. I'll say I'm going to visit Grace, something like that, something that

297

will satisfy them until Phyll comes back."

"I hope all goes well for you," I said stiffly.

"Please, Sheila," Rachel said, "please understand."

"I do understand — it's just that I don't approve." I got rather unsteadily to my feet.

"So you won't be staying to lunch? I can promise you — *no* mushrooms." She smiled, and it was the smile of the old Rachel, the one I grew up with, admired for her dash and daring, for her confidence and warmth and for that special something that so few people have — genuine charm.

Reluctantly I smiled back. At the old Rachel. "Good-bye," I said, "and good luck.

William picked up a copy of the village book from the pile on the table, opened it at the back, and looked at the list of subscribers.

"You do realize that this is the most important thing in the whole book," he said. "I hope you got all the names right."

I smiled. "We were very careful. So, what do you think of it?"

"Quite excellent. You must be very pleased with it."

"The printer did a really good job. But, actually, I only did the history bits and chose the items, all rather fun. Mary did the hard work — all the boring stuff."

William closed the book and looked at the picture on the jacket, which was of the village in its rural setting, with a view along the village street leading up to the church — charming and picturesque. Then he turned to the dedication. " 'For the people of Mere Barton, past and present.' Yes, that's right. It's not the landscape or the historic buildings that matter; it's the people. The community — to use a word I particularly dislike — people acting together, or, indeed, *not* together, but all part of a whole."

"All involved in mankind," I said. He looked at me and I smiled. "Yes, I heard it — it made me think. About Annie, especially."

"Oh yes, Annie. I take it you have solved our mystery."

"Well, yes, I have, but I can't —"

"I don't want to know. Besides, I feel somehow that a kind of resolution has been found."

"Yes."

"Good. 'A broken and contrite heart, O God, Thou wilt not despise.' " He spoke very softly so that I could hardly hear the words. Then he went over to the decanter and poured the sherry. We both sat down and he raised his glass. "To absent friends."

I hesitated for a moment and then raised mine. "To absent friends," I said.

ABOUT THE AUTHOR

Hazel Holt was a personal friend and literary adviser to Barbara Pym, and is Pym's official biographer. A former television critic and features writer, she lives in Somerset, England.

The employees of Thorndike Press hope you have enjoyed this Large Print book. All our Thorndike, Wheeler, and Kennebec Large Print titles are designed for easy reading, and all our books are made to last. Other Thorndike Press Large Print books are available at your library, through selected bookstores, or directly from us.

For information about titles, please call:
(800) 223-1244

or visit our Web site at:
http://gale.cengage.com/thorndike

To share your comments, please write:
Publisher
Thorndike Press
295 Kennedy Memorial Drive
Waterville, ME 04901